# Jonah's Doorway

John Street

To Julie
Enjoy going through
the Doorway
John
—x—

For Jan, Adam, Luke, Jonah & Leah,

you are my world.

# 1

Standing with his back to the window, Jonah faced the blank, barren wall that backed onto the walk-in cupboard on the landing. He could feel a small drop of moisture rolling down his pale face and the freckles that swept across his nose and cheeks. Quickly, he wiped it away with the back of his hand. He had suffered so much pain during these last few years that hiding his feelings came naturally to him. In fact, his tears usually struggled to see daylight. Today was different. It marked the anniversary of his life's darkest memory.

It was either sheer coincidence or a welcome miracle that Jonah had found a way to escape and hide from the things that tormented his soul. Now, more than ever, he needed to be in his favourite place of solitude and comfort. He stood, staring patiently at his bedroom wall, waiting for the strange, piercing light that always transformed the bland, magnolia wallpaper into a surreal 'something' he could never quite explain to anyone else. He just knew if he stared hard enough at the wall, it would appear.

He did not have to wait very long for the powerful shaft of bright light to come bursting through the window and start to burn an image onto the wall, one that Jonah had seen many times before. Gradually, it expanded over the plain wall: a large stately door that stretched from floor to ceiling and was at least five feet wide. It was magnificently carved with precious jewels embedded in the thick metal surface, bronzed, and burnished. The edges of the door shimmered as though trimmed with fire, and as it swung open, inviting Jonah to enter, he could see a bright yellow and white glow from beyond the entrance, making it almost impossible to see what lay in front of him.

Jonah stood, waiting for the breeze that always followed. He felt it swirl around his bedroom in magnificent waves, curling over but not breaking the few simple possessions that he owned. He wasn't scared. He knew the routine. He was ready and prepared to follow the breeze and step through this wild and mystical portal. His own private Doorway. Once through the door, it was a simple and quick journey along mysterious paths. They enabled him to move silently through the hidden infrastructure of his home town, saving a fortune in bus fares, but more importantly hiding and protecting him from his biggest fears.

The other side of the door, whenever he entered, was always full of light. There was no distinction between ground and sky, no noise from living creatures or man-made objects. Jonah had previously overcome this unnerving challenge of stepping through the Doorway, not knowing if he would fall through an empty void beneath his feet or be tightly held in the grip of an invisible force. He had become familiar with the strangeness of this new world and comfortable in this hidden place, once he had uncovered a way to use his Doorway as a portal to explore other destinations.

Today, though, he did not want to explore. Instead, he sat, very still, in the peace of this empty void. Jonah remembered the day his dad left home for good: the shouting and screaming from his mum begging him to stay. It was almost pitiful to watch how she offered to change the way she looked, how she'd behave, all her dreams, just to make him happy - as if it was her fault that his dad had started an affair with a younger woman at work. Jonah felt helpless. He couldn't stop his mum crying or his dad from leaving. This was his doomsday, when his family was torn apart. Now, alone, he relived those painful memories. For a rare moment, secluded and protected by his portal, he allowed the tears to flow.

***

As the days and weeks passed, Jonah vowed he would never allow himself to cry over his feelings again. His journeys through the Doorway were no longer for comfort but simply to keep a low profile and avoid the place where he lived. The estate was not a safe place to be. Self-preservation was high on his agenda: to keep away from those who could and would, given the opportunity, hurt him.

The journey through the bedroom wall usually only took a few seconds and Jonah had become used to the territory beyond the door. Emerging from an open space in front of him was a long white corridor, full of shafts of light streaming past at speed-defying pace, and glass doors sporadically spaced on the left and right. Through these clear panels, Jonah could identify various locations in his town as he passed by. There was usually a door, which led out to a passageway next to his school; a door that took him behind the fish and chip shop; and a door that opened to the entryway next to his Nan's house (which always caused him problems, as he often tripped over the wheelie bins kept there).

However today, a few steps past the portal entrance, Jonah noticed a significant structural change. The white corridor and glass doors had vanished. Instead, a new pathway stretched before him, as far as his eye could see. Brightly lit from underneath, it guided each new step he made. As he began to walk along the path, he could see several strangely distorted objects and shapes come hurtling towards him from distant space. Squinting to see more clearly, Jonah tried to focus on what was approaching. His senses were confused. As they came closer, he thought he could identify some objects that belonged to locations in his home town and outlines of the people he sometimes saw at the supermarket. Then, to his amazement, he began to recognise other figures, some with famous faces; people he had only seen before in history books, or on the television.

This new experience of the portal pathway was at first uncomfortable for Jonah. It broke his usual routine and he was a little nervous about the strange sights floating in space in front of him. However, his keen interest in history (his favourite subject at school) helped Jonah identify major events that had taken place in the past. Recognising the iconic image of an astronaut, next to an American flag firmly planted on the moon's surface, Jonah knew that he was looking at Neil Armstrong on his maiden trip to the moon in 1969. The astronaut was heading straight towards him. Then, without slowing down, he passed swiftly by, only six feet from Jonah's right shoulder. Meanwhile, on Jonah's left side, was a plump man with a dicky bow tie, Cuban cigar and the distinctive homburg hat that identified him as the famous politician, Winston Churchill. Jonah turned the other way and saw a large, bearded man, dressed in lavish golden robes, seated on a throne, looking exactly like the famous king Henry XIII he remembered from pictures at school.

What was happening? A trip that normally took seconds was turning into a journey through the centuries of time. Jonah had lost all fear and discomfort by now. He was fascinated by what he was seeing, revelling in this amazing new adventure.

'Jonah!'

He heard his name in the distance and wondered which of the historical figures was calling out to him.

'Jonah!'

The more he listened, the louder the voice became. As the word echoed and boomed through the portal, Jonah quickly realised this was not part of his new experience. It was his mother, Beth, banging on his bedroom door and shouting at him. It was an urgent call for him to return, sharpish.

***

Outside the bedroom door, Beth was furious. Frustrated at the lack of response from her son after shouting at the top of her voice, she started to yell, 'Have you been to the shop yet?'

No reply.

'Jonah, have you been to the shop yet?' she said again, her voice now rising to a high-pitched screech.

She must not see the Doorway, Jonah thought. Without any preconceived knowledge of how to get back to his bedroom from the portal, he squeezed all his concentration into focussing his mind on where he needed to be. In the blink of an eye, he found himself back there, collapsed in a heap on his bed. Two seconds later, his mother appeared in the room. Slightly puzzled by this experience, Jonah quickly gathered himself, put his fingers through his brown, stringy hair, and tried to sit up straight.

'Erm sorry mum, I was just on my way and I, well, I sort of fell asleep.'

'Don't expect any tea then. I'm fed up with you not pulling your weight around here. I'm tired too, you know, but I never get time to rest.' Beth sounded weary, her throat painful from all the screeching and yelling.

Jonah felt a twinge of guilt. 'Sorry mum. I'm coming now.'

He stood up, heading for the door and, as he passed his mum, put his hand on her shoulder, looking into her eyes. She had beautiful eyes that used to sparkle and beam but now they always seemed so clouded and distant.

'I'm sorry,' he said again, quietly.

# 2

Jonah and Beth moved into their new house three years ago, not long after Jonah's father had left home. His dad had decided he was bored with being married, that he was not fulfilled any more. He thought Beth was focussed too much on her work and not paying him enough attention at home. So, when he met a younger woman in his workplace, he chose to chase after her rather than commit to his wife. After a while, he was not able to hide this new relationship from Beth and the arguments between them became more intense. One day he shouted that he could not think of any reason for them to stay together and left.

Jonah could not forgive him for that: he believed that he should have been a good enough reason for his dad to stay. He hated him for walking out. Not only did the separation cause emotional distress and pain for Jonah and his mother, but it also left them in serious financial difficulties. Although the new house was much smaller than their old one, they no longer had his dad's income. Now Beth had to hold down two jobs to earn enough money to cover all the bills. At first, only eleven years old, Jonah was too young to work but, as the years passed, he began to show interest in finding a part-time job. Without much success. Even now, having turned fourteen and grown to five foot ten, he still seemed small for his age as he often hunched his shoulders through low self-esteem. With his slight frame, he found physically heavy jobs difficult, and his low self-esteem made him stumble over words when asking shop keepers for work. It always ended with rejection. Their financial difficulties did not help with Jonah's wardrobe either. He often had to wear cheap t-shirts and trainers as his mum could not afford the ones with brand names, and his ripped jeans were about an inch shorter than they should be on his legs.

Life was not looking good for Jonah, or his mum. The stress of trying to survive made them both frustrated and irritable. They would throw sarcastic words at each other, tempers fraying and erupting into bouts of angry shouting. It was rare that they ever found time for caring conversation. To keep the arguments from escalating, Jonah spent most of his time locked away in his bedroom. Here, he felt safe.

From the first time that they walked around the new house, Jonah found that he was unusually drawn to a specific room upstairs, which he successfully negotiated with Beth to have as his bedroom. Here he spent hours sketching characters from his favourite animations, the Japanese Anime, with their brightly coloured, vibrant characters and action-packed plots – so different from his own world where he only ever wore dark clothes - black, blue or grey - so that he would not draw any attention to himself.

The move to the new home brought a new dynamic into his Jonah's life. In fact, it started only a few weeks after their arrival. He remembered it vividly...the day he discovered that, tucked away in the corner of the room, was a point on the wall where the special Doorway would suddenly appear from nowhere and, just as suddenly, disappear again. It left nothing but a pale stain on the dingy wall.

The first time it happened, Jonah was petrified. When the powerful light burst into the room and etched the image of the majestic door across the wall, he felt as if his whole body had been frozen. He was unable, and unwilling, to move towards it. Then, slowly, curiosity began to rise within him. What was it? Why had it suddenly appeared like this? Whilst thinking this, a sudden, fierce gust of wind blew in through the open window and lifted Jonah off the ground, gently nudging him towards the door. Then a growing sensation overtook him as he realised that he was being given a choice. He could stand before this door and it would open for him...but only if he wanted it. How he knew this, he never really could explain. He just knew, deep within, it was the case. He was being offered the chance to travel on a journey and he could choose whether to enter through the door, or not.

Eventually, Jonah's curiosity was stronger than his fear. He reached out his hand to turn the handle and the door flew open. As he walked through the Doorway, it took him on a journey, the first of many over the next few weeks and months. Soon he became dependant on it as a passageway to use for secret shortcuts to school, the library, or the local shops. It had become his safety net, his security zone, his escape from reality.

Today, however, in response to his mum's demands, Jonah braved the harsh reality of the concrete jungle that was typical of his local neighbourhood. He took the boring route to the local corner shop, which was not that near – about a fifteen minute walk each way from his home. He wished he could be travelling through the Doorway instead. On those magical journeys, he didn't have to go past the town gang, who were feared by everyone. Now, as he walked along the grubby pavement, Jonah focused his thoughts on his mum, how sad she had become, how life for each of them had changed. He could see no way to avoid their present misery and difficulties. He did not even bother anymore to keep up with social media on his old, cracked pay-as-you-go phone. There was never enough money to top it up, and it was rare he could find anywhere with a decent wi-fi signal. So, what was the point? He had to put up with enough bullying at school. Why put himself out there, just to invite the on-line jibes of his classmates?

His only comfort in the world came from his regular trips through the Doorway. It always made him feel special when it did. He would walk through this supernatural gateway, as though he was the king of the portal. He thought he must be the only one in town, possibly in the whole world, to have a personal Doorway like this. Much better than a mobile phone.

He then remembered the unusual journey he had taken earlier that day, just before his mum called him back to the familiarity of his bedroom. On this last journey, he had seen new strange and wonderful things, not just the usual humdrum scenery of his hometown. It was a mystery. He wanted to explore some more, although he admitted to himself that he was a little scared of going back to this new world again. What might happen next? As he walked and thought, then walked and thought some more, he began to feel a rush of excitement about the new experience.

He had to make another journey through the Doorway.

After visiting the store, Jonah strode briskly home, knocking six minutes off his usual walking time. He charged into the hall, almost punching a hole in the plasterboard as he flung the door handle hard against the wall of the porch. Hastily placing the bag of shopping on the kitchen table, he shot upstairs to his bedroom, desperate to go back through the Doorway. He was oblivious to the sound of his mum crashing pots and pans around in the kitchen as she prepared their evening meal, still frustrated with her son's lack of care and support.

\*\*\*

With all his might, Jonah wished that the Doorway would appear again. He was lucky. He was being given another chance, on the same day, to escape. As the light bathed the wall in front of him, he prepared himself for entry. What would happen this time? Would the portal simply provide him with safe passage to the local shops or would it take him on a different journey, perhaps into another world? This latter thought made him stop in his tracks and he felt a brief surge of panic before, once again, the gust of wind forced its way through the window and pushed Jonah closer to the unknown. With just enough strength to fight the fear, he raised his right hand and, as so many times before, the door swung open, inviting him to enter. This was it. No turning back. No giving up. If the portal decided to take him somewhere new today, he would follow. He just needed courage and confidence to take the first step.

He was in. He had done it. A bold smile of pride appeared on his face. The corridor of light had once again been replaced by the glowing path and cloudlike textures around him. Jonah knew straight away that he was not on his usual route to the places in town, but that he was on a path to a new and mysterious adventure.

Just as he experienced earlier that day, the famous figures from history began to whizz by him on either side: Armstrong, Churchill, and King Henry. This time, though, there were many more glimpses of historical heroes and men of significance, shooting past: the finely chiselled moustache and beard on the face of the

Mongolian leader, Genghis Khan; the distinguished French persona of William the Conqueror; the fierce looking Attila the Hun, the notorious barbarian horseman who pillaged early Europe. All these figures were moving past Jonah as he seriously wondered how far back in time he was going to travel today. As the breeze gathered momentum around him, he thought he must have been travelling a thousand times faster than on his usual trips. He felt an increasing pressure against his body from the wind and could hardly believe he was still standing upright. As he was wondering where this whirlwind journey was going to end, suddenly, without any sign or warning, the historical figures disappeared. Instead, only bright white clouds and a shining path were stretching in front of him as he hurtled through space at breakneck speed.

To his dismay, in the distance he could see an object heading straight for him, at an equally fast speed.

'Oh no, what now?' Jonah said aloud, trying to prepare for what could be a head-on collision with the approaching object.

As the object came closer, Jonah could see that it was a door, in some ways like the one that mysteriously appeared upon his wall at home, but far simpler with no carvings, precious metals or trimmings. Instead, it was made of humble wood, quite small and dull compared to the one in his bedroom. It seemed to be waiting for him, as if it was there on purpose expecting him to bump into it.

There was no crash or bang when Jonah arrived at the door. The wind had subsided and Jonah was able to control his speed and stop in time before he hit it. Cautiously, stretching out his left hand to the door handle, he pushed it gently open and popped his head and shoulders around the wooden frame to peek.

Clang.

'Ahrgggg!' yelled Jonah.

A gleaming double-edged sword dangled menacingly only two inches away from his eyes. It had been stopped by a similar sword that swung down his left side, just in time to intercept the blade and stop it slicing through the centre of his face. Jonah's brain was saying 'run, run' but his body, stiff with fear and panic, kept firmly rooted where he stood. Gripped by exhaustion, his legs felt like jelly and he couldn't do anything except watch and hope he survived.

It seemed that Jonah's arrival into the new world in front of him coincided with a sword fight between two huge men. By their clothing and armour, they looked like soldiers of some kind. Something was not right though. The man to his left was about seven-foot tall and was huge, built like a world champion bodybuilder – but twice the size. His face was shining brightly; in fact, there was a special glow about all his appearance. He was wearing various pieces of armour; a helmet, breastplate, shin covers – all made of solid gold, glimmering brightly like they had been polished to perfection. He had a Roman-style feathered skirt, with gold around each edge, and solid gold wrist protection.

This man was nothing like any other person Jonah had ever seen before. 'Apart from the skirt he'd look great on a skateboard,' he thought, briefly. The soldier swung his sword around his head and, with all his might, directed it towards the neck of his opponent. It was swiftly blocked by the other man's quick reactions and a strong upward stroke of his sword.

Jonah looked at the second man and saw a figure of similar height to the first, only this one was all in black. His full-length hooded cloak covered his entire body. Even his face was disguised by the shadow of his black hood so that Jonah found it hard to distinguish the difference between the edge of his cloak and the start of the apparent gloved hands that gripped his sword. He had a haunted look, dark and harrowing. It was like looking at the image of death portrayed in a scary movie and it sent shivers down Jonah's spine.

One more swing from the first soldier's sword ripped through the cloak of the second soldier, right across his chest. The wounded fighter squealed out in pain, a high-pitched noise that sounded like an eagle caught in a hunter's trap. He placed his left hand on his chest, lowered his sword, and ran off at supersonic speed away from the victorious winner of the fight.

Jonah, still gripped with fear, had not moved from the spot where he had arrived in this strange battlefield. With a strong sense of relief that the scary man had run away, he cautiously turned towards the one who was left standing and slowly lifted his head up to see the bright shining face staring straight back down at him. Jonah's bottom lip dropped as he tried but failed to utter any sound. He found himself speechless.

The stranger, who had won the fight, slowly walked towards Jonah and reaching out his right hand, offered him a handshake.

'You must be Jonah; we've been expecting you.'

How did he know his name? Jonah did not dare to look straight into the man's eyes. Horrified, he thought to himself, 'not today Jonah, not today' and desperately trying to shake off his fear, he slid back inside the small wooden doorway and began to run in the opposite direction.

In no time at all, he was back on the floor of his room. He crawled onto his bed and fell into a deep sleep.

*** 

It seemed like hours, even days, that Jonah had been asleep. He opened his eyes and shot to his feet. He had his fists clenched tight and his body poised in a fighting stance as he scanned the room in search of the two strange men, hoping that they hadn't followed him through the Doorway.

'Phew! It must have been a dream' he thought to himself, and lowering his clasped hands and relaxing his body, he let his body sink onto the bed. Was it a dream, or a terrible nightmare? Did those men really exist or were they an imprint on his imagination of too many game console characters? He sat on his bed trying to make sense of what had just happened.

'Jonah, your tea is ready.'

The words from his mum came resoundingly up the stairs and through his locked bedroom door. Her frustration was still evident in the tone of her voice, and he knew he needed to get downstairs – fast.

***

Tea-time was a strain as they ate their meal in silence. Beth was tired of trying to raise her son on her own. She knew she was constantly nagging him. But what else could she do? She needed his help, especially around the home, but all he wanted to do was stay in his bedroom. It was as though he didn't want to be around her anymore. Beth was convinced this was his father's fault for leaving. Without any more words or looks at Jonah, she sat at the dinner table and stared into space, wondering what had happened to the happy times.

Jonah was too busy looking down, shovelling food into his mouth, to notice how upset and sad his mother was. All he could think about was getting back into his bedroom and going through the Doorway again. What would happen this time? Where would he end up? What if he returned and found those two men still fighting? What if, this time, the sword did not stop short of his face but managed to strike him? Jonah was full of curiosity and excitement, mixed with a hint of terror. The adrenaline rushing round his body made it hard for him to digest his food properly. He finished the meal, hoping it would give him extra energy, and took the plates from the table to the sink. The last thing he needed now was another argument with his mum, so he washed up and cleaned the table as fast as he could.

Beth was still in a daze of her own memories; she hadn't even realised that Jonah had taken her plate away.

'I've got homework to do. I'm going to my room,' Jonah said as he left the kitchen.

Beth only had enough energy to turn her head and watch as her son walked off into the hallway and up the stairs, alone.

# 3

Jonah stood with his back to the window, facing the blank, barren wall, waiting nervously for the wind to arrive. His mind was fixed on the memory of the giant man who seemed to know his name and, although he expected it, he gasped aloud when the familiar shaft of light came bursting through the window onto the wall. The breeze turned into a pulsing whirlwind, swishing and swirling around his bedroom, and the light burned the same image on the wall that Jonah had seen many times before. Once again, the Doorway had appeared.

Jonah entered through the door, slightly more hesitant this time, wondering what was going to happen. The white and yellow shafts of light began to stream by as Jonah moved along the brightly lit path. His heart and mind were in conflict, his head hoping for the entrance to the local shop or library to appear, but his heart longing to return to the battle of the giant soldiers. His heart began to beat faster when he saw the historical characters approaching him again. He was on his way back to the other world: the world of warfare and huge, glistening swords. He shivered as goose bumps appeared all over his arms.

'This is it, now or never, Jonah. I'm not going to run this time,' he said to himself.

He tried to relax and conserve his energy, breathing deeply and allowing his body to move with the flow of the current that was pulling him along. This trip seemed shorter than the last as he looked out into the distance and saw the plain door whizzing towards him.

'This is it Jonah, get ready, get ready,' he said, trying to psyche himself up.

When the door arrived, Jonah was surprised to find that it was firmly shut. He stood there, for what seemed ages, wondering whether it was a good idea for him to try to open it, or if he should just turn around and go back home. Jonah liked to think he was not a coward so he decided to risk it. With an outstretched hand, he began to turn the rusty old door handle carefully, hoping not to disturb anything that might be on the other side. He gently pushed the door away from him and stuck his head around the door for a quick look. This time, there was nothing there. Nothing at all. He decided to go all the way through the door and then jumped with fright, letting out a gasp, as it swung shut behind him with a loud thud. He turned to look at the door and saw that it was firmly closed again. He turned back and had another fright. Standing before him was the skirt-wearing man who seemed even bigger than before. Jonah's mind was whirling with fear and excitement. He remembered running away from this strange man the last time they met. Would he be angry with him for that? Would he shout at him or, even worse, draw his sword? No, surely not, thought Jonah. The soldier had saved his life once before. Surely, he would not hurt him now. The warm smile on the man's face helped Jonah to feel confident that he was not in any immediate danger and he started to relax.

Once Jonah had regained his composure, he said, 'You saved my life last time I was here. Thank you.'

The man stood watching him, with folded arms. The muscles on his chest stuck out like gigantic rock formations. He really was the largest man Jonah had ever seen.

'We are glad you decided to return Jonah,' he said in a bold, strong voice. 'We didn't expect you to leave so quickly the first time.'

'We? Who's we?' asked Jonah, amazed that the man knew his name, never mind the fact that he was expecting to see him.

They seemed to be in a weird place with no land or sea, no mountains or rivers, no towns or cities – just space. Although this was not like the sort of space that you see at night, with millions of stars shining brightly. This space was light and breezy and Jonah discovered he was standing on a spongy swirl of white cloud hovering in the air. This hardly bothered him though. He was much more concerned about how the man standing in front of him knew his name. And where was the menacing soldier who had tried to kill him on his last visit?

'My name is Halecim. I'm pleased to meet you, at last,' the man said.

Jonah looked at him in amazement.

'What on earth is going on? What do you mean, meet me at last…and, by the way, what are you doing wearing a skirt?'

Halecim laughed. 'I was told you would be coming and was ordered to look after you throughout your journey.'

After this response, Jonah was totally alarmed. He could not understand how the man, how anyone, could possibly know he was coming to them through the Doorway.

'This is unreal,' Jonah said, not sure what else to say.

'No, it is very real,' said Halecim.

'But why have you been ordered to look after me?' Jonah said, still in a state of confusion.

Halecim remained quiet for a few seconds, as if pondering how he could answer the question of a young boy with a tiny, human mind.

In a quiet whisper, as though he didn't want anyone else to hear, he said, 'You are in great danger. There is an evil one called Vilde who has requested that he may take you for himself, but my Master wants to give you another chance.'

Jonah was as confused as a chameleon on a smartie box.

'I'm in danger! The 'evil' Vilde! Another chance. Wha-what are you talking about?' he asked, anxiously.

'It will all be made clear as the journey unfolds,' said Halecim.

Suddenly, Jonah remembered the sword.

'Why was the other man here last time, the one you were fighting?'

'He was sent, to, ah …stop you.' Halecim said, as if choosing his words carefully.

'Was he evil too?' Jonah asked, trying to understand the whole situation.

'Yes. Although, he was good, once. Many centuries ago. He was like me, on the same side, before he formed an army of followers who thought they were more powerful than my Master. Then they rebelled and tried to take over His Kingdom.'

'Did they win?' asked Jonah.

'No, they were all thrown out of the city and became the evil enemy of my Master. It's been war ever since. Vilde's chief warrior, Theda, has been sent to stop you.'

Jonah was confused. 'Why didn't your Master just destroy them all?'

'You'll see. In time, it will all become clear,' said Halecim.

The huge warrior leant down towards Jonah and gently whispered, 'Come on, it's time to go. We have a lot of work to do.'

He reached out and held Jonah's wrist, lifting him up and moving them both through the air without walking. Marvelling at this, Jonah was also wrestling with his thoughts trying to get to grips with everything he had just been told.

'I've never heard such a load of nonsense, but could it be true? No, surely not. This isn't real,' thought Jonah.

\*\*\*

Jonah was starting to doubt his own senses. Was this really happening to him? He gradually became aware that he was frightened. If it was true that he needed protecting, why was he still here in this no-man's land, and not returning to the safety of his own world? The last few years had turned him into a hard-hearted boy, forced him to protect his feelings from the problems and pain life had caused him. Back home, he refused to be afraid but here, in this new world, in this strange place he knew nothing about, he was scared. Yet, even amidst all this fear, he had a weird feeling, a sense of belonging. Somehow, he knew this was where he was supposed to be. For now.

They were moving at a fast pace, and as Jonah puzzled over what kind of energy was propelling them forward, he saw that they were coming out of the clouds and heading towards land. It reminded him of when he had been on a plane once, to France on a school trip, and they came down to earth. Here though, the terrain beneath him looked very different from any previous experience.

The view was fantastic: a mountain range that had a steep descent towards a long stretch of deep water, a lake, possibly even a sea. The mountains looked like huge steps going down towards the water and the final step must have been about five hundred metres in length. The land was a rich green near the water's edge, as though life was springing out of the water to energise the shores. There were scatterings of luscious plants, multi-coloured with deep yellows and vibrant pinks. The land to the west was different, a wilderness mountain region. It looked as if it had not seen rain for years, for the ground was cracked and ruined with dirt tracks biting into the dust.

As they came closer to the ground, Jonah noticed a large crowd of people in the distance. Some of them were in the water but the majority were on the shore, sitting or standing on the rocks and sand, observing the activities in the water. Halecim and Jonah landed near the shore, slightly away from the crowd, out of sight but able to see everything that was happening.

'Where are we Halecim?' asked Jonah.

'Don't worry about this place; we'll be coming back in a little while. We need to take a walk first.'

'Where to?' asked Jonah again, wondering if he was going to get a direct reply this time. Unsurprisingly, he did not.

Halecim remained quiet and continued to walk across the rough terrain, following a dusty path.

The amazing scenery and excitement of this new adventure was definitely beginning to wane. The heat from the sun was becoming intense and Jonah was sweating. The sticky moisture on his forehead and the trickles dribbling down his back made him feel uncomfortable. Jonah was not happy that he had to walk, particularly on such rugged, hard ground. He was used to the city life, not having to walk far to get anywhere, especially since he now used the Doorway as his main means of public transport. In fact, he had to admit, he had started to become very, very lazy. Especially if he could use the Doorway to get where he needed to be. Now, he could feel the sun beating down on his head and the pain of his aching muscles.

'Can we stop for a rest?' he managed to pant, squeezing some oxygen out of his tight-pressed lungs.

'We've only been walking for twenty minutes. Why do you need a rest?' Halecim replied. He sounded surprised.

'Why do we have to walk at all?' Jonah said, a little irritated now.

'Ah. Well. Apparently, you have it too easy in your everyday life and so I've been ordered to … open your eyes!'

As Halecim spoke, his lips curved into a strange smile, and his eyes shone as if concealing a hilarious joke.

Jonah was wondering if he had made the right choice returning through the Doorway. Everything that was happening now made him feel very uneasy about the whole situation. He did not understand why this man was here, whether he was really going to protect him, or if the whole thing was a trick.

What if he's on the same side as that other warrior, the one he said was evil? Is he leading me into a trap? Jonah shook his head, as if to shake these ridiculous thoughts out of his mind and remembered that Halecim had saved his life. That had to be good for something. As they kept walking and, although Jonah was more tired than he had ever been in his life, he decided it was best not to moan. Just keep going until they reached their destination, wherever that was.

*\*\*\**

Jonah saw that the sun was beginning to set on his left and so, from that, he knew they were heading north. In the distance, he could see some large rocks but, as they drew closer, he saw that they were not heading towards the rock face but to a small town. A new sense of curiosity overtook his need for rest and a drink.

'Is that where we're going?' he asked.

'Yes. It's a place called Narumscape. We need to follow that group of men,' said Halecim, pointing to a group of about twenty people moving ahead in the distance. They were dressed in full-length garments that looked as though they were once brilliant white but were now spoilt by the dust clinging to them, as their hems dragged along the dry, earthen tracks.

They were men of various shapes and sizes; some looked like they had not eaten for days, others like they ate anything and everything that moved. Jonah easily identified four obese characters at the back of the group, a little isolated as they struggled to keep up with the thinner men in front. Their tunics were tight around their waists and they sweated profusely in the heat. At the front of the group, slightly ahead and making large strides, were three of the tallest men. They were at least a head higher than their companions, thin and scrawny, and needing belts of rope, tied around their waists, to hold their tunics in place. They were the only ones in the group that were clean-shaven. All the rest had magnificent thick, black beards: some meticulously chiselled to a fine point, others left to wander and roam around their owners faces! The wind caught the bigger, bushier beards as the group moved hurriedly along, while the four rotund men who were at the back struggled to follow.

As the men neared Narumscape, they walked down the thin alleyways between the stone and clay brick houses. Each house that they passed had a similar design, square in shape. If Jonah peeped through an open door here and there, he could see that most had four small rooms wrapped around an open courtyard. All the houses had a flat roof and empty spaces where Jonah thought you'd normally expect to see double-glazed windows. He had never seen a house, never mind a whole town, that was so simple in its design and missing many structural 'basics' like two storeys, a sloped roof and, of course, windows!

The group continued to weave their way through the narrow paths that separated the square houses, until they reached the largest structure in the town.

It looked like it was made of the best quality stone the builders could find, with grey marble columns outside.

'This is their local meeting place,' said Halecim.

By now, the group of men ahead of them were entering the building that was already filled with crowds of people. Jonah and Halecim kept a short distance behind the group and entered too. Inside were more marble columns dotted around the large open room, and a cobblestone floor. Jonah glanced around as the other people squeezed into the building. He recognised some of the men that they had followed and observed that the rest of the room was full of other similar bearded men, young and old. They were all focused on a man, on a podium surrounded by pillars, who was speaking. Meanwhile, Halecim slipped to the far side of the room and Jonah squeezed his way around the back of the group to be with his protector, both hiding in the shadows in the corner, out of sight. Jonah wondered how nobody had noticed a boy in a twenty-first century tracksuit and a seven-foot tall bodybuilder, but his main concentration was directed towards the man who was speaking from the podium. He couldn't put his finger on it but there was something different, a little strange, about this man.

'Who's that?' he started to ask.

'Sssh!' was the speedy reply.

The man at the front was talking to his audience, telling them about his father, a different time, and a far-away kingdom; he told stories of people who had lived on the earth thousands of years before. His stories had a hint of realism to them and were very descriptive: some surprisingly violent, full of betrayal and other dark portrayals of horrible acts.

The voice and tone of the man speaking gripped the attention of the audience and kept them listening intently to the imagery and vivid characters he described. Some stories were so fantastic they could easily be made into a Hollywood movie, thought Jonah. The room was quiet while people listened carefully. You could have heard a coin drop on the dusty, clay floor.

'It's a good job there aren't any children here to listen to this gore,' said Jonah, nudging Halecim. 'Who is this strange Storyteller?'

'Storyteller?' said Halecim. 'That's an interesting name for the Messiah, not one that we've used before.'

Jonah did not really understand what Halecim meant by Messiah but preferred his own nickname.

'It's what I'm going to call him. He tells good stories, after all!'

'Shhh! You need to listen,' said Halecim, sternly.

'What is this…school?' Jonah said, almost with contempt.

Halecim turned and stared straight at Jonah, a look that sent shivers down his spine. It seemed clear that Halecim was in awe of this speaker and wanted to listen to every word. He concentrated fully on the words that were spoken tenderly but with the utmost authority. Jonah knew he had been out of line to interrupt, so he turned his head and started to pay attention to the speaker.

The Storyteller was in his early thirties, with a rugged look, as if his face had been caught in one too many sand storms and his hands worn out from the constant use of woodworking tools. He had long, shoulder-length brown hair and a short beard, about three centimetres in length. He was not skinny, nor was he muscular or fat. He had obviously worked hard as a labourer and looked after his weight. His eyes and smile were what made him different to anyone else that Jonah had so far encountered in this strange new world, and his obvious skill was in telling stories.

After a while, Jonah looked around the room and noticed the expressions of deep interest and amazement on the faces of everyone there. That was except for one peculiar looking character; he had sneaked in late and was leaning against the back wall. He seemed very nervous, with a long, thin face and wild eyes that gave him an edgy, almost scary, appearance. He was the only one, apart from Jonah, not looking directly at the man telling the stories. Instead, shoulders hunched, he peered around the rest of the room, scowling. Occasionally, he would turn his face towards the Storyteller, as though wanting to look, but then something strange, almost like an invisible hand, would stop him and he would turn away again. Suddenly, without any warning, he started a manic screeching, in a voice that echoed round the room.

'What do you want with us? Have you come to destroy us? I know who you are.'

Everyone in the room turned and looked at the troublemaker, some shocked that he would dare to interrupt the Storyteller's performance, whilst others mumbled angrily. To Jonah's surprise, Halecim started to move towards the abusive man, his muscles tightening and flexing, and his face tense with anger. He glanced back at the Storyteller who shook his head and slightly raised his hand. Halecim stopped immediately. Then the Storyteller turned his attention towards the wild and screeching man.

'Be quiet,' he said, sternly.

This made some people jump.

'Come out of him,' the Storyteller continued.

At this, the man began to shake violently and, as the people around tried to move away from him, threw himself onto the floor. As he rolled around in the dust, he cried out in pain, then suddenly stopped and lay very still.

Jonah thought the man was dead. The crowd was silent; no-one dared move, or make a sound. Fear filled the air for a while.

After a few minutes, the mood was replaced with anticipation and curiosity as the man on the floor began to lift his arms slowly and an old man, standing close to him, bent down and helped him to his feet. The crowd watched with amazement as the man stood up, calmly. His appearance seemed to have altered drastically and he didn't look scary anymore. The dark, menacing look had gone and he seemed peaceful. The noise in the room gradually grew louder and louder as more people began whispering and talking to their neighbours. Meanwhile, the changed man looked straight into the eyes of the Storyteller, bowed his head, and scurried out of the building.

All was quiet.

Then, one by one, people began to leave the room quickly, keen to go and share the story with the rest of the town. When most of them had gone, the Storyteller also made his way to the exit. As he approached the door, he looked directly towards Jonah and Halecim, smiled, and then left.

They were now the only two people left in the room. Halecim was obviously deeply concerned with what had just happened. His rapid breathing was only now beginning to slow down as he started to relax the tense muscles in his face and body. Maybe it was something to do with the smile from the Storyteller, Jonah thought, but he was quite confused about the whole incident.

'That was a good show,' said Jonah, jokily, as though he had just come out of the cinema and was sharing his opinion of a blockbuster film with a friend.

Halecim turned to look at him, disapprovingly.

'That was not a show.' he said.

'Calm down, calm down, what's your problem?' Jonah said, raising his hands just in case he had to protect himself. 'What's so special about that Storyteller? Why was he shouting at that man who looked like he needed a doctor and a bit of sympathy, rather than being told off in public? He was probably scared of being treated that way. I'm not surprised he threw himself to the floor to hide from everyone.'

Halecim looked at Jonah as if he was perplexed by his casual attitude. 'Didn't you see that something significant and powerful was happening right in front of your eyes?' he said, sounding a little angry. 'This Storyteller, as you call him, is far more powerful than any doctor. He is more than just a man.'

Then with a voice full of authority, more like a command he said, 'I think it is time for you to return home.'

Before Jonah could reply, Halecim had disappeared.

Jonah looked out at the open space before him, confused and puzzled as to why Halecim should be so upset with him. However, he did not want to remain in this strange place any longer without his new protector. He decided it was time to find the wooden doorway to go home, especially as he was hungry and could do with a rest. He glanced around the room and there, in the far corner, was the entrance to the portal that would lead him home.

# 4

The next morning Beth woke in a daze. Just for a moment, she didn't know where she was. Her eyes, still bleary and blurred, tried to focus on the huge, white object in front of her. Then a small smile forced its way to the corner of her mouth as she realised it was just the fridge. She must have fallen asleep, with her head on her arms, leaning on the kitchen table. She felt like she had been in a dream-world for hours but now, back in the real world, she struggled to find the energy to get to her feet. Once she managed to get up from her chair, Beth looked around the kitchen to see what jobs needed to be done first. Although Jonah had cleared away the plates after tea, he had made a total mess of the kitchen. He had only done half the job of cleaning-up.

'Why do I bother?' she thought to herself, as she put on her yellow plastic gloves and began to clear up the chaos so that they could have breakfast.

At this point, Jonah came downstairs, walked into the kitchen, checking the cupboards and then opened the fridge door, looking for something to eat.

'I'll finish your job then,' said Beth, not even looking at her son.

'I haven't got time for this mum,' Jonah said, in a similarly frustrated voice. He really didn't want another argument, especially after his exhausting trip the night before.

'Oh, you haven't got time. You never have time. All you ever do is think about yourself. You don't care about me, you just look after number one, and when it gets too hard, you walk away. You're no better than your father.' As Beth came to the end of yet another angry rant of frustration, her eyes filled up until they could no longer contain her tears, and she began to cry.

'How dare you compare me to him...I am not my father. I am not my father.' Jonah yelled. 'You have no right to do that. I'm not surprised he left home if you were always nagging him, blaming him for your pathetic life.'

Even as the words left his mouth, Jonah realised this time he had gone too far. He knew that his words were like a knife that cut straight through his mother's heart. He was not sure what to do next. When he saw the pain in her eyes, he was filled with guilt but, still, he could not bring himself to say sorry straight away. Something deep inside would not let him admit to Beth that he was wrong. Maybe it was pride. Maybe it was the truth, he didn't know. In a moment of complete helplessness, he ran past his mother, up the stairs to his bedroom. There was only one place he wanted to be, one place that could take him away from his pain and from the reality that he needed to face. The Doorway had become his key to freedom, freedom from his mum, from the pain, rejection and the loneliness that he felt.

\*\*\*

Once inside his room, Jonah began the same routine for entering his dream world of illusion. Fortunately, for him, the Doorway never showed any signs of frustration, even though it had only been ten hours since it last closed. Once again, the Doorway appeared when it was summoned. As he entered through its enticing pathways, Jonah felt the familiar rush, that same feeling of excitement and adrenaline that he felt whenever he began a new trip. Only this time, these feelings were clouded by a dull pain as he remembered the horrible situation he had just left behind in the kitchen.

The new journey started at a slow, almost plodding pace. However, after a while the speed picked up as the ever-familiar visions of episodes in history whizzed by Jonah, startling in their brilliant colours. These glimpses of past events spinning around him, and the promises of new adventures, made him forget about the row with his mum and concentrate on the present moment.

\*\*\*

As Jonah stepped through the old wooden doorway, the sun was rising on the horizon, bright and colourful.

'Welcome back. I didn't expect to see you so soon.'

Although, at first blinded by the sun, Jonah could only see the man's silhouette, he knew straight away that it was Halecim.

'I needed to get away from home, away from...,' Jonah replied.

'What?' Halecim asked, inquisitively.

'From my...,' Jonah hesitated. 'Er, from an awkward situation.'

'Why didn't you deal with it, instead of running away?' Halecim seemed to be pressing for answers.

'Just drop it. Okay. I'm not running away. Anyway, aren't you here to look after me...not question me?'

'You are right. I am here to protect you. Though I don't understand much about you humans, or indeed your struggles. I apologise for suggesting that your problems are simple to resolve. Please forgive me.'

Jonah was not used to hearing apologies of this kind. Although he felt Halecim's words were sincere he also recognised an element of challenge, not just remorse. He thought briefly about this and then nodded his head in acknowledgment.

After this, Halecim raised his hand and pointed behind Jonah. 'We need to take that path today.'

Jonah turned around quickly to see they were no longer standing by the wooden doorway. Instead he saw a winding mountain track.

*\*\**

Beth had finally stopped crying, though her eyes were still extremely red and sore. She could not believe that Jonah had been so cruel, that he had finally said what she always hoped he would never say. He had not been this hurtful with his words before, and it was the first time he had been so aggressive in his denial of any similarities between him and his father. She made her way through to the living room and slumped down in a chair. As she sat there, she kept thinking about the recent argument, replaying it again, focusing on the words Jonah had chosen to use. Why did he say that? All she had ever done was love him and want the best for him. Why was she getting the blame because his dad abandoned them both? Her whole life had been destroyed, broken into pieces by the messy divorce and she felt completely and utterly isolated, without any knowledge of how to deal with, or overcome, the pain.

For the last three years, Beth had brought Jonah up on her own, working as hard as she could to give him everything he needed, and wanted, and trying to be both a mother and a father to him. She had given up all her own hobbies and leisure activities, and her social life had become non-existent. Only recently they started going to the local social club on an occasional Saturday night, just because Jonah had become so bored with watching uninspiring, prime-time television and had convinced her that he was old enough to go. Although she did not feel comfortable in the club, she succumbed to his demands, only to sit in a dark corner of the room with her vodka and orange. She felt lonelier than ever as she watched her son try to enjoy himself on the dance floor. Beth had tried everything, everything she could think of to help him cope without his dad.

Today, as Beth sat in the living room on the creaky fake-leather chair, staring aimlessly at the wall, anger and pain about her situation welled up inside her. She felt she had been to hell and back, all because her husband had walked out on them both. He didn't choose to stay and work out their difficulties together. He took the easy option, packed his bag, and left to be with another woman. Her hatred towards this man had never been dealt with and Beth found that not only was bitterness and loathing strengthening its grip on her but she was beginning to feel negatively towards her son.

# 5

They had been walking for a while when Halecim stopped and made a gesture with his hand, signalling that Jonah should stop too. In the distance was another small group of men, on the edge of a town, walking towards some houses that lay on the outskirts.

'Not again,' thought Jonah.

'Are these the same men? Have we just gone back in time to that last town we visited?' Jonah said, with some degree of frustration.

'No, Jonah, it's a different group. We'll come across many other similar sights. You are not here to look at people's physical appearance but to see how they react to the situations they are in.'

Jonah wished Halecim would stop talking in riddles and be clear and straight with him, but he didn't want to moan anymore. Instead, he decided to keep quiet and do as he was told. For now, anyway.

The group they were watching suddenly stopped in front of them. There was a slight commotion as a strange-looking man stumbled towards them, dragging himself along the ground. He seemed off-balance. Although he tried to use his arms to stop himself from falling, his hands were only stumps, with no fingers. He wore an old, ripped, and torn blanket, wrapped around his body as if he was trying to cover every limb and keep them out of sight. Jonah watched closely as the group tried to move away from the approaching man. They shuffled their feet and vigorously pushed and pulled at each other, trying to be as far away as possible. Jonah wondered why they didn't just run if they were that scared. What was happening to keep them rooted in the same place? His curiosity kept him focused on the situation as he tried to understand the reason for the strange behaviour from a group of fully-grown men.

Then someone familiar at the back of the group caught Jonah's eye. 'Where have I seen him before?' Jonah thought for a moment before the memory came rushing to his mind.

It was the strange teller of stories he had heard on his last visit, who had commanded the wild man rolling around on the floor to be still. This time, he was standing behind the group as the rest cringed in their attempts to avoid the blanket-covered man approaching them. The fascinating Storyteller stood tall, unmoved, and unafraid. He must have been watching the whole incident and the way he looked at the men showed Jonah that he was not at all happy with the contempt that they displayed towards the beggar. He began to walk slowly through the group, staring into the eyes of each one, as if disappointed at their childish behaviour and complete disrespect for the struggling man.

'What's going on?' Jonah asked Halecim, impatiently.

'The man in the blanket has a very serious disease. The other men think that they will catch it too, if he gets close to them.' Halecim replied.

'Why don't they just run away then, or ask the man with the stories, you know, the Storyteller, to shout again?'

'Because they would never shout at the man who they call Master. He is far more powerful than any man and has powers nobody has ever seen on earth before. Instead they fear 'the Storyteller' as you call him. They follow him because they think he is different to anyone they've ever met before. They admire him but they are still fearful of him, not truly knowing what he is capable of.'

This made Jonah curious to see more and he joined Halecim in moving closer to the group so they could hear what was being said. The strangely diseased man began to speak nervously to the only one who would look at him. He seemed afraid of what the response might be but was courageous enough to mumble a few words. Now on his knees, in front of the Storyteller, he stretched out his arms towards him.

'I know that you can make me better sir, if you want to, so p...p...pl.. please do.'

One of the men in the group picked up a stone and threw it at the man on the ground, shouting, 'Go away, you filthy, evil leper. Leave our leader alone.'

The stone narrowly missed both men, so another stone was picked up. Some of the other men in the group followed. They also picked up stones. They obviously had no thought of the consequences if a stray, misguided stone might hit their leader. The diseased man was terrified and clung on to the Storyteller's feet with his stumpy hands, trying to hide from this unprovoked attack. The bombardment of stones was fierce but, somehow, they all missed the two men, flying inches either side of them but never actually hitting them.

With an impressive movement, the Storyteller raised his right arm up towards the crazed, stone-throwing men. His fingers pointed towards the sky and his palm was aimed at the angry mob. They looked afraid and began to cower, stumbling as if pushed backwards by an invisible force, which was so strong it lifted their feet off the ground and threw them to their knees. One by one, they dropped their stones, yelping with pain as if their hands were on fire.

Everyone watched the stones tumble to the ground and explode into clouds of tiny particles. The frightened men stared at the smouldering heaps in front of them, hugging their wounded hands, not knowing whether to run away or stay. The beggar-man looked astonished, moved by the awesome sight but more than that, by the Storyteller standing by him, to protect and stand up for him.

Jonah thought that probably no one had ever supported the beggar before, let alone fought his corner. He admired the Storyteller, especially when he turned to the beggar and calmly said, 'I do want to help you. Be clean!' Then, he gently touched the man's mutilated hands. Instantly, the disease left. The man stood, staring in amazement, at the full set of new fingers on his healed stumps.

The stone-throwers, some of whom had regained enough strength to return to their feet, were amazed too. Not only had the Storyteller blown them away, literally, he had touched the untouchable. Now they muttered statements of disgust:

'This is unheard of!'

'Not in our land.'

'Men with diseases like this are outcasts...filthy, unclean people.'

'They must be evil. That's why they're cursed with a lifetime of suffering.'

'What on earth is going on?'

Today, in front of the scoffers, the Storyteller had dared to touch one of these outcasts.

Although Jonah was interested in what had happened, he was less bothered about the healed hand, which he suspected was probably an illusion anyway, than the look on the Storyteller's face. It reminded him of something. Someone. A face. It was one that brought back memories, too many memories. It was a face full of compassion and love, a painful reminder of how his mother used to look at him, when he used to fall over, or told her that he had failed another school test, or been beaten up by the other boys.

It had been a very long time since Jonah remembered anything good about his relationship with Beth. The last three years had been mostly filled with hurt and rejection, and Jonah always felt the need to blame Beth for his father leaving them. Now, in this moment, he remembered a time that made him feel particularly miserable. He had just started secondary school and was struggling with a barrage of bullying at school because he had to wear a brace on his teeth. He was the only one with a piece of metal stuck to his face and his 'friends' were extremely cruel about it. The brace looked hideous, a terrible sight that Jonah hated. He did whatever he could just to keep away from school and, as a result, fell behind with his education. He was considered by the other pupils as the 'joke' of the school, pushed to the fringes of the playground, befriended by no-one.

He remembered that dreadful day when he could no longer cope and decided that his life was pointless and he would be better off dead. The only way he could imagine ending his life was to jump off the local railway bridge. He thought if the fall didn't kill him, then a speeding train would. He remembered how he stood on the bridge, waiting for the next train to come. A passing stranger had called the police and a massive commotion was caused as roads were blocked, traffic was stopped, and crowds of adults and children gathered in the distance to see what was happening. The railway bridge was only a short distance from the school, and many teachers and pupils joined the growing crowd of onlookers. Some of the boys who bullied Jonah shouted for him to jump, although they were immediately removed from the scene by the teachers and a police officer who stood near them. Still, the bullies' words reached Jonah's ears and he knew they were right. He was a failure, a boy with a pointless existence, and he knew he could not live without being needed and loved anymore. His world had fallen apart, his dad had left, no-one liked him, and he couldn't cope with the pain anymore. Yet, the only thing that stopped him from jumping off that railway bridge was the look on his mum's face as she stood at the police roadblock, reaching out her hand and telling him that everything would be alright; that she loved him and that his life was worth more than this. She would help him cope. She would help him get through all this.

When Jonah saw that same look of compassion and love in the face of the Storyteller, he found he could no longer control the tears that began to stream down his cheeks, so he just let them flow.

'Are you alright?' Halecim asked. The soldier seemed unsure about what he should say or do. He put his hand on Jonah's shoulder and glanced over in the direction of the Storyteller, as if looking for inspiration or instruction.

The Storyteller, however, was watching the beggar run into the town, shouting at the top of his voice that he was cured. Before he rushed off, the Storyteller had asked him to go to the local priest who would verify the diseased man as 'clean' and then he would be allowed back into town. He asked the man to keep his experience quiet and simple, but that was never going to happen. Instead, the man was shouting with exuberant joy. So, the Storyteller began to move away from the attention of thrill-seekers who were queuing to see yet another supernatural happening. Turning towards the group of men, his so-called followers who still looked terrified, the Storyteller took a step towards them. They all flinched, moving aside to form an aisle for him, while he walked straight through the middle of the group. No words were spoken. Everybody watched the Storyteller walk away and then, when he was at a safe distance, followed him.

An increasing noise was escalating from the town, coming from the direction that the shouting man had gone.

'We need to move,' said Halecim. He seemed unsure whether to disturb Jonah or not, but they could not stay any longer as a new crowd was already on its way to follow the Storyteller.

Jonah looked up at Halecim and gently nodded, letting his protector lead the way. Their pace was not very fast, but that was hardly surprising considering the rough terrain and the amount of energy that Jonah had expended during their last journey. As they walked, the only sounds that could be heard were their feet kicking small rocks lying on the rough ground, and the distant hum of voices from the crowd who were looking for the Storyteller.

Neither Halecim nor Jonah spoke as they kept on walking.

***

A few hours after leaving the town, they reached a cave tucked into the rocks, close to the path they had been following. The wind was picking up and starting to blow dirt and sand into their faces. It was time to find shelter. Just inside the entrance of the cave were two rocks where they sat, facing each other.

They were silent for a few minutes before Jonah spoke his thoughts aloud. 'There was something different about the Storyteller this time. It was his face. That look...on his face. It reminded me of how my mum used to look at me, sometimes.'

Halecim sat and listened intently as Jonah continued.

'Before I came back through the Doorway, I had an argument with my mum. I just couldn't hold back my anger. I said some things to her that were bad, very bad. I hurt her, you know. I've never been good at sharing my feelings or using the right words and this time I went too far. When I was younger, I used to get treated like that diseased man - not that I had a disease or anything, but I was different from the other kids. Every time I was hurt or upset, mum would reach out her hand and look straight into my eyes. Her face was always filled with love, just like the Storyteller's face back there.'

Halecim was attentive, as if fascinated by this outpouring of human emotion. 'Do you think it helped, seeing the man healed?' he asked.

Jonah looked surprised. 'What do you mean…healed? That man can't have been healed just by someone speaking or touching him – don't be ridiculous.'

'You didn't see his fingers growing back?'

'I s'pose. But it must have been a trick of the light, an illusion, or something else. These things just don't happen.'

Halecim bowed his head. He seemed frustrated by this reaction to his question, disappointed that Jonah had dismissed the thought of the man being healed.

Again, they sat in silence, deep in thought in their own separate worlds. The cave where they rested was narrow at the entrance and the light from outside allowed Halecim and Jonah to see each other's faces dimly, but not distinguish between the shadows around them. At the back of the cave was a wider, more open space but, without any light shining from anywhere other than the entrance, it was impossible to know which living beasts had made the cave their home.

Suddenly, Halecim sensed the presence of something that should not have been there. He looked towards the depths of the cave. It was troubling him and he looked increasingly concerned for their safety as he pressed his left hand down on the rock and placed the other hand on his sword…waiting. His muscular arms flexed as he slowly pushed himself to his feet. His biceps begin to twitch and his hair was ruffled by a swift movement of air that swept through the cave. His eyes adjusted to the darkness around him as slowly and methodically he scanned the area, looking for something that did not fit the shape of the cave. The hollow expanse was calm and still, but Halecim looked as if he knew something else was present, something that was a threat. He continued to move carefully, going further into the deep and the darkness, constantly scanning the area for any sign of movement.

Jonah felt uncomfortable that his protector was no longer by his side. He tried to call out to Halecim but, when he opened his mouth, no words came. Although this worried him, he decided instead to make his way carefully towards the darkness, hoping he would find his protector there. He felt a nervous sweat dripping from his forehead as the tension grew. Where had Halecim gone? He placed his hands on the wall of the cave, groping his way towards the darkness. A worrying notion came to him that this was a bad idea. However, he kept inching his way, step by step, deeper into the cave.

Suddenly, as if from nowhere, a huge and powerful hand came from behind his neck and covered his mouth, pulling him backwards. Jonah felt a warm breath blowing on his right ear.

'Don't move.'

Jonah sighed with overwhelming relief as he recognised the voice. It was Halecim.

Fear was never an option for Halecim, it seemed. Perhaps it was because he was not human but he never displayed any signs of panic or alarm. He quietly kept looking backwards and forwards, still trying to see what was in the cave.

'Down,' said Halecim suddenly, pushing Jonah to the floor of the cave. With his right hand, he grabbed the glistening hand-carved handle of his sword. It was drawn from its sheath in an instant and raised towards the ceiling of the cave. Halecim then stepped in front of Jonah to shield him from whatever was about to happen.

Clang.

It was that sound again, the ear-splitting noise that Jonah had heard when he first entered this ancient world. Fear gripped him as he realised it was Theda, Vilde's chief warrior, coming back to get him.

Jonah cowered against the wall of the cave and slipped into a crack in the rock face. He could not see Theda, as there was still no light, and however hard he tried, he could not see Halecim either. All he could see were yellow sparks as two swords struck each other, hard, creating glimmers of light. All he could hear was the high-pitched, deafening squeals of the warrior fighting with Halecim.

Jonah was unaware of his protector's full range of powers, whether they included night-vision, or any other ability to see in the dark. He presumed they were able to fight it out by using instinct alone, but now was not the time to ask.

The two soldiers somehow knew the precise position of where each other's blade would cut through the air, at lightning speed. They sped around the cave, jumping against walls and boulders that littered the floor of the cave. The swords clashed providing frequent, if brief, bursts of light that allowed Jonah to keep track of where the soldiers were. Then, rather abruptly, it stopped.

All was still and quiet in the cave.

Jonah scrunched his body tighter against the crack in the wall, trying to make his presence invisible. The fear of being taken by Theda made him tremble; even more, the waiting and uncertainty of what was going to happen next made him feel sick. He tried to focus his eyes into the darkness and looked around the cave.

Nothing.

Then it came - the loudest scream Jonah had ever heard, reverberating with full force around the cave. It was Theda, heading straight for him.

Jonah stopped shaking. He kept his eyes tightly shut, not wanting to see this beast approach him. The sound of the squeal was deafened by the two swords hitting each other again, right in front of Jonah's face. Halecim had trapped the warrior's sword against a rock that jutted out of the wall, just above Jonah's head. Jonah could feel Theda trying to move his weapon but Halecim had pushed down hard with all his strength and, without warning, punched Theda in the stomach. As Jonah opened his eyes, he saw Theda reeling from the punch as Halecim swung his sword around, forcing it down the left-hand side of his enemy's head and body, slicing a large gash on his hand. Furious at the loss of his sword,

Theda squealed even louder than before and, with drops of black blood dripping from his wound, he disappeared.

All was silent for a few seconds. Then Halecim grabbed hold of Jonah's shaking arm, which was hugging his head, and pulled him out of the cave. The piercing daylight hit Jonah as they reached the entrance and he squeezed his eyes tightly shut again.

Halecim kept moving at an awesome speed across the land, dragging the bewildered Jonah with him, until they found some shelter near a river. He continued to scan the area for Theda, while Jonah sat behind a rock. It was time to catch his breath and calm his nerves after this frightful ordeal.

'Are you okay?' Halecim asked, still looking around.

'Yeah. I'll be alright.'

There was a pause.

'How did he know we were in that cave?' Jonah asked.

'Because you do not believe,' said Halecim, as though the answer was obvious.

'What do you mean...I do not believe?'

'Theda's master, Vilde, succeeds when people doubt. He feeds on scepticism, and he is drawn to the power of disbelief,' said Halecim. 'You have dismissed the Storyteller and the things you have seen as foolish and imaginary. So, as the scent of your unbelief grows stronger, it means his warriors, especially Theda, will find it easier to locate you.'

'What a load of ...,' Jonah began, in a voice of contempt, but he was swiftly interrupted.

'Be very careful what you say. This is not a game…it is real. Your choice of words is becoming very dangerous to your wellbeing. And to mine.' Halecim was stern and his tone was sharp.

'I need to get out of here. This is messing with my head,' said Jonah.

'I think you are right. Your Doorway can be found to the left of that rock.' Halecim pointed to a slab, twenty feet from where they sat.

Jonah stood to his feet and began to walk towards the rock. 'I'll see you soon, Halecim. And, by the way, thanks for saving my life again.'

As Halecim watched Jonah leave, he couldn't help but smile.

# 6

Jonah stood outside the local community centre and took a deep breath.

'Do I really want to do this?' he thought to himself.

After a few tense breaths, he pushed the door open and walked inside.

'Can I help you?' asked the woman sitting behind the reception desk.

'I'm looking for the gym.'

'Straight down that corridor and left at the end,' was her reply.

'Thank you,' Jonah said, as he made his way nervously down the corridor. He had spent a lot of time thinking about Halecim's warning that Theda was coming to get him. He did not really understand what Halecim meant about his disbelief drawing the enemy closer, but he was concerned that the evil warrior may return when no-one was there to protect him. Jonah tried to relieve his worry by remembering the last part of the fight and saying to himself, 'Theda was once dangerous, but now he's quite 'armless!' This made him chuckle.

With Halecim as his bodyguard and protector, Jonah certainly was not scared about returning through the Doorway, but he wanted to prepare himself. He needed to learn how to fight his own battles and he thought the local boxing club was the best place to start.

*** 

As he opened the gym door, Jonah peered inside first, scanning the room to see if anyone was in charge. He didn't feel comfortable walking into an unfamiliar room, especially without his personal warrior standing by his side. The room was filled with various pieces of equipment and boys and men hitting punch bags and lifting weights. There was a strong smell of sweat from the hard work that each was putting into their training, and certainly not a hint of fear in the air. These were all muscular, hard-fighting human weapons.

The centrepiece of this fighting world was the boxing ring: a roped-off area where two people would fight to the end. Jonah's imagination ran riot as he pictured himself in the ring with Theda. There he was, bobbing and ducking away from the soldier's sword, jabbing Theda in the back and in the ribs as he swiftly moved around the ring. The evil warrior swung his sword towards him but constantly missed as Jonah moved like a butterfly, weaving in and out of his opponent's legs, eventually kicking him and knocking him off balance. As Theda lay on the floor, Jonah dived in for the kill, dropping down to the floor and smashing his elbow into the dark, hooded face of his enemy. Winner!

'First time here son?'

Jonah jumped with a start, still in his dream of the glory fight in the ring, and only half hearing the deep voice talking to him.

'I'm sorry, what did you say?' Jonah asked.

'Is this your first time in a place like this?' the man repeated.

'Yes sir.' Jonah was fumbling for words. 'I was just looking at the ring.'

'Ah. Everyone who walks through this door looks at that ring and thinks about their first fight. And you know what everyone has in common?'

Jonah shook his head.

'They all win!' said the man, smiling.

Jonah tried to deny that he was the same as everyone else and that he wasn't really thinking of his triumphant battle over an evil warrior. Somehow, the man did not look convinced.

'Would you like to step in and have a look around or are you going to stay holding the door, letting in a draught?' said the man. 'By the way, my name's Kyle.'

So, this was Kyle. Jonah had heard a lot about him. He was the manager of the local boxing club and had been a world champion boxer for three years running. Kyle was easily six feet tall and looked to Jonah like he was in his early thirties, young enough to have no wrinkles and a 'youthful' appearance, but old enough to seem mature and wise, as though he had been through a lifetime of tough experiences in, and outside, the ring. He had a thick mop of black hair, which was trimmed and well groomed. Kyle obviously looked after himself physically; he could easily have been cast for a role in a men's moisturising advert. His face was not beaten or bruised in the way Jonah thought a world champion boxer might have been. To look at him, he didn't look as if he could hurt a fly. His smile made Jonah think of a caring and tender primary school teacher, but he knew that everyone in the area showed a great deal of respect for Kyle and all feared his ability to knock a man out with a single punch.

Jonah decided to follow Kyle into the gym. He felt very strange, as though everyone was looking at him, and he was a little awestruck by the thought of this gym becoming the place where he could learn to be a champion. As they walked around the room, Kyle described how to use the different pieces of equipment to develop muscles and core strength. Jonah tried to take it all in but he was only interested in getting into the ring and fighting Theda.

'As this is your first time, we will take it slow to begin with. We don't want you injuring yourself before you've even thrown a punch. So, what's your name kid?'

'Jonah.'

'And why do you want to learn to box?'

'I want to be prepared.'

'Prepared for what?' questioned Kyle.

'Prepared for when he… when he…' Jonah went quiet, unable to finish his sentence. He knew how stupid it would sound if he tried to describe fighting Theda, the evil Vilde's chief warrior.

'Being prepared is a good start, but revenge and anger is something that needs to be fought from the inside. Learning the art of boxing will teach you self-discipline, control, respect, and inner strength. Whatever demons you face, here you will learn to overcome them from the inside first.'

Although Kyle was a world champion boxer, he did not seem arrogant or boastful. He spoke these words with a deep wisdom, almost as if he knew what Jonah was planning. But, how could he? Surely, he did not know about Theda. Jonah was intrigued.

After Kyle showed Jonah around the various sections of the gym, he began to take him through an introductory course, which included skipping, sit-ups, and weight lifting. Jonah threw himself wholeheartedly into this training session and, by the end of a gruelling hour of exercise, he was ready to collapse.

'Well done, Jonah. You've done well for your first session.' Kyle looked pleased. 'We'll build your training slowly at first, as your muscles will ache for a few days. See you again next week?'

Jonah walked home with a massive smile on his face. He was feeling as though he was invincible, as if nothing could defeat him, a new sensation for him. It was great. As he walked along the pathway, he re-lived his imaginary great battle in the ring, punching the air as he moved from side to side along the pavement. He chose to ignore the occasional twinge of pain as his muscles hurt from this unfamiliar experience of vigorous exercise.

He was looking forward to his next session.

\*\*\*

Beth was sitting quietly at the dining room table that was already laid for tea. She looked tired, worn out and not very happy to see her son.

'If we had a dog, your dinner would be in it,' said Beth quite sharply, as Jonah walked through the door. 'I don't know why I bother,' she continued.

Jonah saw the half-empty bottle of vodka on the table and decided it wasn't worth trying to explain where he had been. They would only end up arguing again. Whenever his mum had been drinking, all she wanted to do was shout at him and blame him for pushing her husband away, for making her life seem worthless and pointless. It was getting harder for Jonah to convince himself that it was the alcohol making his mum talk like this, or that she didn't really mean the things she said. He stared at her, feeling a mix of emotions: pity, compassion, and despair.

He used to enjoy meal times when his dad was with them. It was always the same routine, but he liked that: fishfingers on Monday, chicken, rice and peas on Tuesday, pizzas on Wednesday, some form of pasta every Thursday and on Friday, fish and chips. Best of all was Sunday lunchtime, when they had a joint of lamb, or beef, and sat around the kitchen table together.

Now, there seemed little point in eating as a family. Food was just something Jonah had to eat to survive and he would rather miss a meal than sit with Beth in one of her moods. Jonah shrugged his shoulders, resigned to an empty stomach, and climbed the stairs to his room.

Beth was too drunk to realise that Jonah had walked off. She continued to mutter and murmur under her breath until her head slowly slumped onto her arms, balanced on the table beneath her. As she did most nights now, she quietly cried herself to sleep.

***

Jonah sat on his bed thinking about Theda. He was becoming obsessed with his experience in the cave and his last conversation with Halecim. Coming home from the gym, he thought he could fight the whole world and win. But was it all about muscle and strength? After his work-out session, Jonah felt strong, but as he walked through the front door of his home, he knew he did not have the power to cope with his mum. His insight and understanding were weak and he was unsure how to change that into inner strength. Halecim talked about belief and feelings, and Kyle had said that he had to fight from the inside, but what did all that mean? Jonah was deeply confused. Would he have to fight the evil warrior and could he really win? Even if he did, what would be the point of winning battles in Halecim's world and losing them here, against his own mum? It was time to go back through the Doorway and get these questions answered.

# 7

The familiar journey began and Jonah's mind was so pre-occupied with his thoughts that he didn't realise he had already reached the exit door. A deep, strong sound startled him.

'I thought you weren't coming back?' said a very familiar voice.

'Well, I couldn't leave you to fight all the baddies on your own, could I?'

'Oh, believe me,' replied Halecim, 'I am not on my own. Far, far from it.'

Jonah was curious to know what Halecim meant but decided this was not the time to question him. There were other answers he needed first. 'Where are we now?' he asked, looking around at a cluster of windowless houses.

'Don't you recognise it? We are on the north shore of Streegenna, in the town called Narumscape. We approached it from the far side last time and ended up in their local meeting place.

'Oh yeah, where I first heard the Storyteller,' said Jonah.

'Well, the one you call the Storyteller has just arrived back from his travels to neighbouring towns and villages.

You have some questions and we are on our way to get some answers.'

Jonah was excited. At last.

Halecim led the way into town as Jonah tried to keep up with his protector's massive strides.

\*\*\*

They walked along the perimeter of the houses until they found a pathway between two buildings that led them into the centre of the town. As they grew closer, Jonah recognised the sound of excited, happy voices with lots of chatter. Turning a corner, they joined the edges of a large crowd of people gathered around the doorway of one of the houses in the street. What was going on? Why was everyone so excited? There was a mix of people of all ages, young and old, rich and poor, all trying to get a look inside the house. It seemed obvious to Jonah that the poorer, lower social class of people were stuck at the back.

Halecim was looking around as though he had something, or someone, that he wanted to see. After a short while, he patted Jonah's shoulder to get his attention and pointed to a group of men coming along the road towards the house. At first, Jonah thought they were just four ordinary looking men with scruffy beards and long curly hair. Then he noticed something strange. Each was tugging at the corner of a large mat carrying, between them, a fifth man, who was presumably unable to walk for himself and looked very embarrassed as everyone watched him. The group struggled along the road, changing hands repeatedly, as if worried that the mat would slip through their sweaty palms, trying desperately not to bounce their friend around on the knitted trampoline!

'You need to pay attention to these men, particularly the one on the mat,' said Halecim.

Jonah watched as the men arrived, exhausted, at the back of the crowd. They tried to push their way towards the house, to reach the front door and get inside, but nobody would let them pass.

'Have a heart,' said one of the men. 'Can't you see he's paralysed?'

Some people shrugged as if they didn't care. Others did not take too kindly to being pushed out of the way. Everybody there wanted to see what was going on inside the house. Nobody wanted to give up a place in the queue. Disappointed, the men gently lowered their friend on the mat onto the ground, then huddled together to work out a plan of action. Jonah could hear snippets of what they were discussing; they seemed determined not to let a simple crowd problem stop them getting to where they needed to be. They picked up the man on his mat again and headed towards the back of the house. Jonah, curious as ever, was about to follow when a large hand grabbed his shoulder and pulled him back.

'We will get a better view from inside,' said Halecim.

\*\*\*

In the blink of eye, without even feeling that they had moved, Jonah found himself inside the house, standing next to Halecim at the back of the main room.

'How on earth did we get here?' said Jonah, completely amazed.

'When are you going to start believing? You are watching an event that happened two thousand years before you were born, and all you can ask is how did we get into a busy house?' Halecim was baffled at Jonah's lack of intellect. 'Just look around and see what is happening here.'

At first, Jonah could not see very much, so he moved to his right and followed the gaze of those around him. All eyes were focused on the Storyteller. Jonah tried to hear what was being said, but the loud hum of excited chatter in the room made it difficult. Then someone hissed a loud 'shush' and the noise began to quieten down. At this, the Storyteller stood in the middle of the room and began to tell more of his stories.

'What's he saying?' whispered Jonah, not sure he understood the gist of each tale.

'He often describes things that resemble the lives of the people he is speaking to,' said Halecim, making sure he kept his voice low. 'Sometimes he will talk about shepherds on a hill, or growing crops in the field, or the struggles these people have with the laws of their land.'

'I get that,' said Jonah. 'But why is it important?'

'Because these stories have hidden meanings, which are easy to uncover if people really want to know the truth.'

Jonah was not sure he was bothered about the meaning behind the stories, but he did enjoy listening to the Storyteller's voice as he described the characters in his fables and imaginatively brought them to life. The rest of the audience looked fascinated too.

Suddenly, something small and hard hit him on the forehead. Startled, Jonah looked up to see little bits of stone falling from the ceiling. Those around him also felt the stones and the Storyteller stopped speaking. As people began to look upwards, concerned that the roof was about to collapse, a bright ray of light appeared in the room, streaming through a hole that had appeared in the ceiling.

The hole grew bigger and bigger.

'What's happening to my house? Who's up there?' shouted a very angry man.

Obviously, the house owner, thought Jonah.

The angry man was trying to push his way through the crowd to go and investigate but the Storyteller stopped him and whispered something in his ear. This seemed to calm him down. Then, everyone watched the ceiling with great anticipation, to see what would happen next.

After a short while, a head became visible through the hole in the roof. A man, who Jonah recognised straight away as one of the four carrying the mat earlier, looked around the room until he saw the Storyteller. He smiled and then lifted his head back up again, out of sight. There was a moment of quiet and then, slowly but surely, the mat appeared through the hole and was lowered down on cords, still supporting the paralysed man, into the middle of the crowded room. Those watching began to voice their different opinions about what was happening. Some thought it amusing that these attention-grabbers had ripped a massive hole in the roof, while others clicked their tongues in strong disapproval.

The men on the roof reached as far down as they could until the mat reached the chest level of the Storyteller. He was watching them all with a massive smile on his face. The man on the mat was blushing with embarrassment and started to apologise, hoping that the house owner was not going to hit him, but when he looked into the eyes of the Storyteller, he started to relax.

'You obviously have some friends who care very deeply about you,' said the Storyteller. 'They believe that I can help you and have risked their lives, in a very creative way, to place you before me. My son, your sins are forgiven.'

Then, the Storyteller placed his hand on the man's forehead.

A loud cheer came from the men on the roof. They wanted to jump for joy but did not dare let go of the cords supporting the mat, in case they dropped their friend on the floor!

The whispers and murmurs in the room began to get louder as people began questioning what had just been said.

Jonah whispered to Halecim, 'Why are the blokes on the roof happy? Surely, they didn't carry their friend all this way, and wreck the roof, just to have a few words spoken to him. Don't they want to see a miracle or something?'

'They just have,' said Halecim. 'Watch those grumpy looking characters over there. They are the religious leaders. Do you see how angry they are getting?' he continued.

'Yes, but why?' asked Jonah.

'Because this man has received the most precious gift in all of earth or heaven.'

'What's that?'

'Forgiveness,' Halecim replied. 'And these religious leaders are so wrapped up in their own thoughts about how good they are that they have stopped remembering that forgiveness is a gift. They think it's something you earn by being righteous.'

'What does righteous mean?' asked Jonah, confused.

'Obeying the law. They think that by simply doing what is recorded as right in the law books, they will earn a place in the Great Kingdom,' Halecim continued. He sounded irritated.

Jonah was still confused. Halecim was talking nonsense again, he thought. He was about to express this when something else in the room caught his eye. The man on the mat had been helped down to the floor by some people in the room and he was now beginning to move. He began to drag his left leg over the surface of the mat, whilst slowly swivelling his right leg around to join it. With both legs pressed together, he bent his knees. Supporting himself with the help of his arms, he pushed his weight onto his legs and slowly began to stand up on both feet. In wonder, he shook his legs as though there had been nothing at all wrong with them. There was a gasp of shock and amazement from the audience in the room, and from the roof, when the man bent down and picked up what had been his bed.

'He hasn't been able to do that for twenty-three years,' shouted somebody from the crowd.

The healed man seemed in a daze. He rolled up his bed, humbly turned to the Storyteller, said thank-you, and began to walk out of the house. Gradually, the tightly packed crowd parted and made a path for him to squeeze through. The only noise that could be heard was the shuffle of feet and the movement on the roof as the man's friends quickly made their way down the outside stairs to greet him. As the man left, there was a strange silence in the main room. Nobody knew what would happen next. What was the Storyteller going to do?

After a short while, the silence was broken by a shout of anger, 'Who's going to fix the hole in my roof?'

Halecim grabbed Jonah's arm.

'It's time for us to go.'

\*\*\*

Jonah could see the town from a distance. They were on a nearby hill, looking down on Narumscape. Jonah watched the large gathering of people milling around the house where they had been just a few seconds before. Halecim was walking on ahead of him and making his way up a hill.

'Hey, wait a minute,' Jonah shouted.

Halecim kept on walking.

Jonah tried to catch up. 'Hey!' he shouted, trying to make Halecim stop. Eventually he did.

'I have some questions that need answers. You said I was going to get answers,' Jonah said, angry now.

'Oh, well, I'd better answer you then, before you get really angry and hurt me,' said Halecim, as if through gritted teeth.

'I didn't know you could be sarcastic.'

'It seems that there is a lot you don't know,' said Halecim, even more sarcastic now.

'Okay. Let's start with why you keep taking me to freak shows with that Storyteller,' said Jonah.

'How dare you call them freak shows? You are witnessing events that have changed the course of history and provided humanity with an opportunity to survive. The man you insist on calling 'Storyteller' saved the disabled man's life and, by the way, his spiritual life too.'

'But how? With just a few words about forgiveness? And how do you know that the man couldn't walk before and it wasn't all just a show?' said Jonah.

'You sound just like those religious leaders. Think about what you have seen so far. The man in the meeting place who came in completely out of control and left calm and subdued. Think about the man with the blanket and the withered hand, remember, the one the crowd tried to stone. And think about the man lowered down on the mat. Can't you see? All these men had something wrong with their mind or their bodies, but they had something far worse troubling them – their souls were dead. And that is what the Storyteller was dealing with.'

'I'm sorry, I just don't get it. It doesn't ring true with me,' said Jonah.

Halecim seemed frustrated that Jonah did not understand. 'Then you will need to see more.'

'No. No, I don't want to.'

'I'm not giving you a choice,' said Halecim. 'There are things happening in this world which have a significant effect on the life you're living back home. You can't ignore things in the past because you don't understand them or because you don't think they are relevant to you now, in your present. Once we've finished our journey through time together, and you have seen everything I need to show you, then you can decide what you want to believe.'

Jonah was struck by the degree of authority in Halecim's voice. He knew he needed to follow his new protector, whether he wanted to or not. He also recognised it would be best for him not to complain or moan as that would only frustrate and annoy Halecim even more. The last thing Jonah wanted to deal with right now was an angry, muscle-pumped giant. It was like being at home and learning when to ignore, or challenge, his mum.

Halecim led Jonah to a large lake. They had been here before. Jonah recognised the hustle and bustle of market traders selling their crafts, pottery, food and clothing. Fishermen were mending their nets and getting ready for their next fishing trip. Today, many people gathered around those telling anyone who wanted to hear about their tales of adventure, or read from scrolls, or shouted out prophecies of doom.

Halecim, however, led Jonah to follow a large crowd of people who were walking in the same direction as they were, along the shore of the lake. They were drawn by a familiar voice, the voice that always put a smile back on Halecim's face. It came from a man who was talking to the crowd about his father, unseen kingdoms, and how the people needed to change the way they lived upon the earth. His voice was soft and smooth but full of power and authority, and Jonah knew that, once more, they had found the Storyteller.

The sand sloped down towards the sea, which was very calm and peaceful. The sun shone in a blue sky, completely clear of clouds or flying birds. There was no wind, not even a slight breeze in the air, nothing to carry the Storyteller's voice across the large gathering of people. Somehow, everyone still seemed to hear what he was saying.

Halecim and Jonah stood at the top of a ridge on the shore, looking down towards the edge of the water where the crowd slowly walked behind the man who had grabbed their attention. A stream of onlookers kept steadily joining the procession, either because they were excited about the Storyteller's message or because they felt they were missing out and wanted to be part of this growing phenomenon.

'What are we looking at, exactly?' asked Jonah.

'Just be patient!' said Halecim.

'But you always say that. We always stand and watch, until someone approaches the Storyteller with a problem. Is it going to be the same again?' Jonah was becoming bored with all the waiting around.

'You are in this place for a reason,' said Halecim, testily. He did not seem very impressed with Jonah's attitude. 'It is no accident that you found the Doorway and ended up here. To understand what is going on, I therefore suggest you put a little more effort into paying attention to what's happening right now.'

Jonah took the hint and kept quiet. He let Halecim lead him closer to the Storyteller, as they both wound their way through the crowd without people noticing or blocking their way.

Suddenly the procession came to an abrupt halt. Some people ahead had stopped and now stood to attention, as if ordered by a sergeant major's shout on a soldier's parade. Jonah was puzzled. He could not see any reason for anyone in the crowd to stop until he realised that they had taken their cue from the Storyteller. He was standing by a small table, covered with piles of silver and gold coins. Behind the table, a stocky man with an oily face sat looking at the Storyteller with a broad grin on his face. He was well dressed and his beard was neatly trimmed.

'That's a sign of wealth and influence,' Halecim told Jonah.

Although the man at the table seemed happy, the people reluctantly handing over money to him were unfriendly, even hostile, towards him. Halecim explained that this man was a tax collector, taking money from the people to hand over to the ruling powers, the Romans, who had overtaken the region and now demanded high taxes. As this tax collector was a fellow citizen of the people in the crowd, they saw him as a traitor, the lowest of the low, as he worked for their enemy. Why should he benefit from the oppression of his people, whilst taking a share of the profits for himself? In other words, he was a legalised thief.

Murmurs of outrage spread through the crowd when the Storyteller stopped to talk to this man. A wave of criticism and disbelief filled the air. How could the Storyteller, a man they all respected and admired, even consider talking to this thief, this collector of unfair taxes? Whether the Storyteller knew the people were thinking this or not, he did not show any concern about their feelings of disgust. Instead, he looked straight into the tax collector's eyes and said:

'Levi. Leave all of this and come, follow me.'

Without a second thought, the tax man stood up, left his table full of money, and began walking with the Storyteller.

'Have you eaten? Please, you must come to my house for a meal. Please, you must come.' Levi was so obviously excited and overwhelmed that the Storyteller had spoken to him, let alone asked him to follow him, that he could not stop blurting out his persistent invitation.

To everyone's surprise, the Storyteller agreed and walked with Levi towards his home. Immediately the crowd began to follow, all curious to see how this meeting would develop.

Halecim led Jonah away from the crowd, taking him through the backstreets of the town to the house where Levi lived. It was a large, rectangular, single-story building with arched windows, and an open lounge area filled with coloured cushions and bright decorations. This extravagant home was an obvious expression of wealth. Halecim told Jonah that Levi was a corrupt man who had legally stolen money from his own people to feed his selfish desires, increase his wealth, and live in luxury.

The two onlookers did not have to wait long before an over-excited Levi led a procession of friends, colleagues, and followers of the Storyteller into his home to celebrate. As he did so, he constantly announced that today had been his own personal miracle.

'I'm not sure what I am supposed to be watching for here. Do we just stand around watching people eat, drink, and get merry?' Jonah was genuinely confused.

'Sometimes we need to see the whole picture,' said Halecim, 'to understand the painter who has painted the canvas.' Then he pointed towards the window. 'And here is the final stroke.'

A group of men outside the house were leaning in through one of the window openings. These men were also finely dressed and obviously wealthy. Halecim explained that they were the high-class, religious elite who normally took centre-stage in any public gathering. By the expressions on their faces, they now seemed envious that they were not invited to this particular party. They summoned two of the Storyteller's followers over to the window and began to question them quietly about their leader's decision to share his time with this unclean man.

Although the Storyteller was deep in conversation with some of Levi's friends on the opposite side of the room, he somehow heard every word that was being said at the window. After excusing himself from his own discussion, he turned towards the window and spoke to the room in a loud voice.

'Teachers of the law, guiders and advisers, you who have been given the honour of showing the people how to live a good and worthy life, pleasing to my Father, and yet you ask why I am here in the house of Levi, sharing time and food with tax collectors and 'sinners'? Surely you should know it is not the healthy but the sick that need a doctor; it is not the righteous people who need to spend time with me but those who need to be forgiven.'

The religious leaders looked down at the ground, as if they were naughty children 'told off' by a school teacher, and slowly shuffled away from the house, embarrassed and ashamed.

Before he could see anything else, Halecim tapped Jonah's arm and suddenly they were both whisked away, in a brief moment's journey through time and space, to a hill on the edge of the town.

*** 

In a daze, Jonah looked at Halecim in bewilderment. Although he did not dare to ask again, his face was filled with frustrated curiosity. When was he going to get some answers that made sense of all this?

Halecim seemed to read his thoughts and tried to explain.

'Let's just consider what we have seen today. A sick man was brought before the Storyteller to be physically healed. Instead, he was offered forgiveness. This was far more important to him. After that, he was healed. The people watching didn't understand. And now we have just seen religious leaders judge the Storyteller's choice to spend time with those who are social outcasts and in desperate need, not of physical healing but of the healing of their soul, mind, and spirit.'

Jonah was about to ask more questions when suddenly a familiar noise stopped him. It was the high-pitched scream of Theda approaching from the distance. He was on the chase again. Halecim grabbed Jonah's arm and fled as quickly as he could, dragging Jonah with him. As they travelled at speed through the wilderness, the squealing sound soon disappeared until all was silent. Once again, they had escaped a close encounter with their enemy.

Halecim led Jonah to a secluded area where he found a crevice behind a rock for them both to hide behind. As they arrived, Halecim quickly scanned the area to make sure it was safe before they settled.

'Do you see now? This is what I'm talking about!' said Jonah, impatiently. 'Running for our lives, scared of a stupid monster. Isn't it about time we took him on...end this battle, for the last time?'

'Do you really think he is our only enemy? Do you think that sound was just from one person? There is an invisible army, with millions of warriors at war against my Master, and using humans to win their war.'

Jonah gulped. He could see that Halecim was deadly serious. 'Can you teach me to fight, how to use a sword?'

'You can't fight these demonic forces using only metal. You have to fight them using your head and your heart.'

'But you use a sword. Why can't you teach me? What if he comes when you're not around?' Jonah was getting anxious at the thought he might have to face Theda alone.

Halecim looked as if he was deep in thought. 'Well, it isn't in my brief, but then...no-one said that I couldn't.'

He pondered a little longer before coming to a

decision. 'I will show you enough to defend yourself, just in case I am ever delayed in reaching you.'

From beneath his belt at the back, just below his shoulder blades, Halecim took a sword. It was a small dagger but to Jonah, it seemed a massive weapon, a sign that he was soon to be a man, even a hero. (His thoughts were running ahead of him!) Halecim carefully handed the dagger to Jonah, who took hold of the handle. When Halecim let go, it was much heavier than Jonah had expected. He nearly dropped it but Halecim grabbed it quickly, stopping it from piercing Jonah's right foot. Jonah breathed out a sigh of relief and gestured a motion of thanks towards Halecim who was now helping him to raise the dagger with both hands.

'I am only going to show you the defensive moves. You don't need to attack as I will always be with you before the second strike of the swords.'

Halecim put Jonah into the correct position for a defensive attack, making sure that he had one leg in front of the other, slightly apart, with his weight evenly balanced over both legs. He held Jonah's hands upwards, making sure that his arms were slightly bent at the elbows. Halecim then took his own sword out of its sheath. It glistened and shone in the sunlight, almost blinding Jonah with its piercing light. The huge sword came swooping down towards Jonah's small dagger. Petrified, Jonah stood his ground – whether through an inability to move due to fear, or out of pride and stupidity – and gripping his dagger tightly, he waited.

Clang.

The swords clashed together. Surprisingly, Jonah stayed on his feet and kept hold of his sword.

'Well done Jonah. Not bad for your first go.'

'Wow,' thought Jonah to himself. 'I can do it. I can defeat Vilde's chief warrior.'

Jonah's new self-belief was soon quashed when Halecim added, 'Now I will show you how hard Theda hits.'

With a quick movement, Halecim swung his sword from behind his back and, with all his might, thrust it at Jonah who had to quickly move back into position and take up his stance. He was determined to hold off his opponent once again. The swords met and there was no clang this time but a loud whoosh. Jonah cried out as the strong vibration through the metal burnt his palms and, though he tried to keep hold of it, his dagger went flying out of his hands and into the distance.

'I think we need to work more on your grip,' said Halecim.

Disappointed, Jonah took a long walk to retrieve his sword.

When he returned to the practice arena, they continued. After a couple of hours, Jonah could hardy hold his arms up. He was exhausted.

'I think that's enough for now. We can leave it for today,' said Halecim, his voice full of urgency as he gave his young protégé these words of warning: 'From now on, I want you to think seriously about what is going on here. The battles that you find yourself facing will not be won by the sword, but by the decisions you make.'

Somehow, Jonah knew it was wise advice.

# 8

Sweat was pouring down the side of his head and the middle of his back. Jonah pulled, pushed, and heaved the dumbbells up and down, as he had been instructed to do. The weights were not very heavy but Jonah was not very strong. Kyle was helping him with a balanced routine that was aimed at developing his upper and lower body, but Jonah was only interested in strengthening his arm muscles. He knew that the small blade given him by Halecim was no match for the mighty sword of Theda. His only hope of having an equal fight would be if he could lift a much larger, heavier sword and keep hold of it. He had little motivation for the aerobic exercises or leg muscle exercises that Kyle tried to get him involved with; he only wanted to work on his biceps.

'I'm not interested in running or sit-ups, I just need strength,' Jonah said, forcing out the words whilst gasping for breath as he put himself through the vigorous exercises.

'I don't know who's told you that you win a fight purely by physical strength, but they're wrong,' said Kyle. 'You win a fight with your head, your heart, and your feet. You use your head to outsmart your opponent, your heart to keep you going when all your strength has gone, and your feet to keep you moving…weaving in and out of their attack and running away if necessary.'

As he listened to Kyle's smart words, Jonah began to realise that, without a magic wand, he did not have time to grow big muscles or much increase the size of his biceps. Very soon, he would have to defend himself, to stand up and fight. During his training sessions in the gym, he constantly looked in the full-length mirrors, flexing his muscles and hoping to see any sign of improvement. As Kyle said, he would need to find ways to overcome his adversary other than physical strength. He was starting to feel very uncomfortable and nervous about what the future might bring.

***

Jonah had stopped using the Doorway as a shortcut to get around town, so he made his way back that afternoon on foot. He had found a new respect for his Doorway. He realised it was not an energy-saving portal but a route to discovering a deeper meaning for his life, a purpose for being on this planet. He was excited but also worried that, the next time he used it, he might have to confront Theda. Walking idly along the pavement, Jonah contemplated his training in the wilderness with Halecim and at the gym with Kyle. His thoughts played with the warning both his fight trainers had given him: 'It's not all about physical strength.'

That could be a good thing, he pondered, as he knew his muscles were seriously underdeveloped. 'So, where is my strength?'

He walked along the tired, dirty streets of the run-down estate, a forgotten part of the town's redevelopment plans; new weeds sprouted and grew next to the old, brown-green flora that crept out of the cracks in the pavement slabs. The drains were clogged with wet, rotting leaves and there was rubbish strewn everywhere, all over the public spaces and private gardens. People did not seem to care anymore about the area where they lived. There was no pride or community spirit; people looked after themselves, or kept themselves to themselves, for fear of upsetting the wrong people.

The short journey home from the community centre gym took Jonah past a derelict part of town where nobody wanted to go – the flats. In a town of thirty thousand people, there was only two blocks of high-rise flats. Each had seventeen floors with four apartments on each floor. These flats were designed to house two hundred and fifty people in each, but both had over three hundred residents crammed into the tiny spaces. This was where the poorest, most troubled families, were placed by the town council. Hidden away from the more affluent parts of town, nobody seemed to care about the people who had the greatest needs. Instead, they feared and ignored them.

After this street, known by locals as Ghetto Street, Jonah passed the local park. This was a neglected mud-

and-grass pitch with the remnants of a children's play-area covered with poor attempts at graffiti. Uninspired, bored young people with felt pens (none could afford spray paint) scribbled misspelled tag names and pseudonyms, to protect their identities from the police. Someone had set the lonely swing on fire and the burnt rubber seat was melted out of shape and uncomfortable for anyone to sit on. There had been a solitary bench where parents used to sit and chat about their daily lives, while their children played happily together on the climbing frame. Now it was wrecked by local youths trying to create some kind of entertainment. Young families never used the park anymore. The empty bench was a depressing reminder that this park was no longer a place of fun.

As he walked past the normally deserted park, Jonah was so caught up in his thoughts that he was unaware of his present surroundings. Suddenly, something moving to his right caught his attention. He turned to see a man slowly push himself up from the splinter-ridden park bench and move towards him. This shifty looking character wore a scruffy, black coat that reached down to his knees; a pair of black jeans that were ripped in four places due to wear and tear rather than a fashion statement; a pair of yellow-white, stained trainers; and a crop of messy grey-black hair which was curly at the ends and very greasy. He did not look particularly healthy and was bursting out of his clothes. At first, wrapped up in his own thoughts, Jonah did not recognise who the man was, although he did seem familiar. Then, as the figure drew closer, Jonah felt a rush of confusion followed by revulsion and a surge of anger.

'What the hell are you doing here?' he demanded.

'Now, that's no way to talk to your dad,' said the man who had walked out on Jonah and his mother three years before.

There had been no contact made during those years, no Christmas or Birthday cards, no texts or emails. He had left nothing behind but pain and hatred and now he had the audacity to appear out of nowhere and act like nothing had happened.

'You're not my dad. You're nothing to me except a distant memory.'

'Now son, that's...'

'Son! You lost the right to call me that the day you walked out and deserted us. I don't know what you're doing back in town and I don't care. So just crawl back to wherever it is you came from.'

Jonah's father looked genuinely surprised; the force of such a strong rebuke and rejection seemed to knock him back. He gave a faint smile and tried a new tactic. 'Come on Jonah. Don't you want to know why I've been sitting here, waiting for you?'

Jonah had already begun to walk away; his shoulders and head bent towards the ground. Hearing his father's voice made him deeply angry but he stopped and stood very still.

'I've met this amazing man,' his father said. 'He's my friend now, and he's really made me think about the way I –'

'Stop. I don't want to hear it,' said Jonah, cutting his father off mid-sentence and scowling with deep hatred at the man he no longer recognised. Speaking with a voice that grew louder in volume, he continued, 'I don't want to know why you've come here…and I don't care about your new friends. You had your chance to have a life with us but you blew it. You got bored with mum and me, so you left us to set up home with that other woman! You threw us away like unwanted objects, with no thought about how we'd feel… how you were tearing our lives apart. Now, you're dead to us. I don't ever want to see your face again.'

Jonah's dad stood in silence. It was clear from his trembling chin that these words had hit him hard.

For a second, Jonah wondered if this was because his words were exceptionally cruel, or if his dad, perhaps for the first time in three years, realised what he had done to his family. Jonah quickly dismissed this thought as of no concern to him now. All he could feel at this moment was rage. Above, the sky seemed to match his mood: turning grey as darkening clouds quickly merged to threaten a heavy storm. At the rumble of thunder, Jonah began to walk away, leaving his bedraggled father standing alone in the pouring rain.

\*\*\*

89

As he returned home, Jonah reflected on his anger towards his mum and his dad. The difference with his mum was that he loved her and hated to think of how much pain he was causing her with his outbursts. The intense guilt that he felt stopped him from being brave enough to say he was sorry, to apologise for his cruel words, and hope that she would forgive him. The longer that time went by, the harder it was to face her.

Hoping, once again, that he would not have to walk directly past his mum to get to his bedroom, he began to turn the handle on the front door. His recent encounter with his dad had not put him in the right frame of mind to say sorry to Beth. Not at this moment. He was far too angry to suppress his emotions and he certainly did not want to explain to his mum what had just happened.

Fortunately, on this occasion, Beth was nowhere to be seen. Jonah went straight upstairs to his room and closed the door behind him, dropping his wet gym bag on the floor by his bed. Soaked through and dripping from the unexpected torrential downpour outside, Jonah crawled onto his bed. He was physically and emotionally drained. After his training session at the gym, Jonah had begun, for the first time in ages, to feel positive about his life. Now, that all seemed a distant memory. His arms, neck and face muscles were tense. He could feel his blood pounding in his heart, not from the heavy physical workout but from the seething rage that he felt after his shock encounter with his dad.

Cold, wet, and shivering, he started to shake, increasingly losing control. He had never experienced such physical convulsions before. What was it? He could not stop it. He didn't understand it. He was scared. As far back as he could remember, he would cry out to his mum whenever he was truly scared. Not now. Not this time. Everything had changed and only one name was on his lips as he cried for help.

'Halecim.'

# 9

The journey through the Doorway happened much quicker than usual this time. It appeared that a cry for help to his guardian was enough to stir the Doorway into action and, soon enough, Jonah was beginning a new journey down his personal pathway. He did not even remember moving from his bed towards the wall, let alone the strong, loud, forceful wind that pushed against him seconds before he reached the wooden door into Halecim's world.

'Jonah, what's wrong?' Halecim reached down to help him to his feet. Jonah had arrived through the portal hunched up on the floor in a slumber. His legs were weak and wobbly so, to help him stand, Halecim held both his arms firmly until Jonah had stopped shaking.

Staring into his protector's eyes, Jonah could not keep the tears from forming as Halecim repeated his question.

'What is it? What's wrong?'

Jonah stood looking at his friend but no words came. He had no desire to speak, or the energy to describe what was wrong to a supernatural warrior who usually did not seem to understand human emotions anyway.

However, Halecim did seem aware that his young companion was struggling with some strong emotions he could not describe, and focused his attention on getting Jonah to a safe place, to rest and recover from whatever had happened moments before he came through the Doorway. He gently put his right arm around Jonah's waist and whispered, 'Hold on,' before speeding off north westwards, towards the mountains.

They arrived at a small cave, near the mountain summit. Having thoroughly checked out the whole of the cave this time, Halecim placed Jonah gently on the floor, laying his head on a smooth rock, and sat close to him, blocking the draught that came in through the entrance, keeping him warm whilst he slept.

***

In his dream, Jonah was struggling with wild thoughts and imaginings. He was on a quest to find the answer to a very important question. What was it?

He found himself on a beach following some footsteps in the sand and he could hear the lapping of waves in the distance. As he walked, he could hear fragments of the words Halecim had shared with him on a previous journey.

'There are things happening in this world which have a significant effect on the life you're living back home.'

What things?

In his dream, Jonah kept on walking as several images flashed into his mind: a man who was lame beginning to walk, or a hand withered to a stump now planting crops in a field. Images of men who were busy, happy, alive.

The voice of Halecim kept whispering, 'Can't you see? They had something much worse troubling them than their illnesses. Their souls were dead.'

Then Jonah found himself in a boxing ring, punching into the air; not hitting another boxer but something invisible. It was the dark memory of his father's face staring at him in the park, drenched by the rain.

'You can't ignore things in the past because you don't understand them.'

Halecim's voice kept filtering into his mind. Something about these journeys back into the historical past connected Jonah to his father in the present day. He was sure of it. Jonah continued to follow the man in the sand, longing for him to turn around and look back at him. He had a feeling that this man was the one who could answer all his questions. Finally, the stranger turned his head and Jonah gasped. He was looking straight into the face of the Storyteller.

***

While his young ward slept, Halecim kept watching intently the entrance of the cave, fixing his eyes on the small amount of daylight that squeezed through the entrance hole in the rock. A breeze ruffled the giant's long, sun-bleached hair as he sat waiting.

After a while, Jonah began to stir from his deep sleep. Unsure as to where he was, as all was dark in the cave around him, he called out in a loud whisper to his friend.

'Halecim.'

'I'm here,' the reply came.

When Jonah began to move, Halecim moved away to give him room to move and prop his back against a rock behind him. Once Jonah had orientated himself and recognised that he was once again with his protector, he realised that his journey following the Storyteller across the sand was just a dream. He felt hugely disappointed, as he still had no answers about why he felt so troubled when he saw his father in the park. Did he hate his dad, or did he secretly hope he would come home? Jonah felt confused.

'What is it?' said Halecim.

'Nothing. Just a dream.'

'Do you want to talk about it?'

'No. Can you take me to the Storyteller?' said Jonah.

'Why?' Halecim was surprised at the lack of friendliness and jokey banter that Jonah normally shared with him.

'I need him to answer my questions.' Jonah was not prepared to go into detail.

'Well. It's not as easy as that,' said Halecim.

'I don't care how easy or difficult it is. Just take me to him.'

'Be very careful Jonah, I may have been ordered to look after you but do not confuse 'guide and protector' with 'slave' or taxi driver!'

'Look Halecim. No disrespect. But I think you must have some close connection with the one you call 'Master.' I think he has something to do with me being here. Otherwise, why do you keep showing me what he can do with his 'special' powers? I don't think it's just you bringing me through the Doorway. So, I need him to answer my questions, not you,' said Jonah. 'Actually, I believe the answers I need are way above your pay grade!'

'Well, I suppose it's about time you believed something!' said Halecim with more than a hint of sarcasm.

Suddenly, without any word of warning, Halecim stood to his feet, grabbed Jonah's left arm (a little too tightly for Jonah's liking) and whisked him away at lightning speed. How they managed not to hit their heads on the rocks as they flew out, Jonah did not know. Somehow, he didn't care anymore. All that mattered to him was to understand why his meeting with his dad had caused him so much turmoil.

They moved so fast that Jonah had no time to identify any of the villages and towns that they passed. It was all a blur, until Halecim reached his destination. This time there was no gentle, progressive slowing down on arrival. Jonah had upset Halecim far too much to expect a comfortable landing.

Thud. Jonah hit the ground hard.

'Ow,' he cried, as his arm scraped the floor. The sudden pain came from a splinter. A piece of battered wood had pierced his hand. Jonah sat up quickly, leaning his back against a frame behind him, as he fussed over the palm of his hand, using his thumb and fingernails to pull the splinter out. He then carefully pressed another finger over the cut to stop the small bubble of blood from flowing. Once he had finished performing like a 'drama queen' over his little wound, Jonah began to assess his surroundings.

Surprisingly, Halecim was nowhere to be seen. This was strange. He had never left Jonah alone before.

For a moment, Jonah was worried but soon he became distracted by his growing need to find the Storyteller. He also became aware that he was rocking gently from side to side. Peering up and over the wooden object that he was leaning against, Jonah discovered that he was on a fishing boat in the middle of a huge lake. There were many other smaller boats following but this boat was in front, the furthest from the shore. Jonah was at the stern, the rear part of the boat, hidden behind a crate. As he peered over the boxes and fishing nets, he counted twelve men hustling and bustling around in front of him. Most of them had big bushy beards and masses of black, curly hair. They all wore long, white, flowing garments with a simple V-neck collar. The only difference between their outfits was that some of the men had deeper shades of dirt splattering their robes. Each wore patterned belts, wrapped tightly around their waists to keep their hems from dragging on the floor. On closer inspection, Jonah recognised some of the same men who were at the tax-man Levi's house party, on his last visit. They were friends of the Storyteller. Jonah felt a thrill of excitement. That must mean that he was here too.

Jonah bobbed his head up and down from behind the crate, trying to keep hidden but keen to locate the Storyteller. It was difficult to see much amongst all the upturned crates and activity on board, but finally he saw him. Tucked away at the front of the ship. Jonah could hardly believe it. He was lying down, fast asleep on a large cushion. Jonah tried to move carefully, making his way around the pile of smelly, scale-filled fishing nets, towards the Storyteller. He hoped that the other men would not see him, as they had never noticed him or Halecim before, but this time it was different.

'Who are you?' said one of them, gruffly.

'What are you doing on our boat?' demanded another.

'How did you get here?' said another puzzled voice.

Jonah was just as surprised as they were. He was no longer invisible. It must be because Halecim was not with him, he thought. It then occurred to him that if these men could see him, so could the Storyteller.

'I need to talk with the one who's sleeping at the front of the boat,' said Jonah, feeling surprisingly brave.

The men stared at him in amazement. They had never seen a boy with such a pale skin, and strange clothes so different from the local fishermen they knew. They were obviously shocked that this alien stowaway had managed to climb on board their boat, and even more surprised that he now demanded they should wake their Master from his sleep.

'He can't be woken up, just to talk to you,' said a tall, skinny man, angrily.

'Listen,' began Jonah, 'this is very complicated. I won't go into details as you won't believe me anyway, but I have some urgent questions that need to be answered and that man over there is the only one who can help me.'

Gasps of disbelief and stirrings of angry emotion began to grip the sailors.

'Who do you think 'that man' is?' asked one of the taller men.

Without hesitation, Jonah replied, 'I think he's just a bloke who tells stories and heals a few people but, for some reason, my friend thinks he has some special powers. So, I think, maybe, he can answer some of my questions.'

The sailors began to grow restless. They looked as if they were ready to throw Jonah overboard for his outrageous statement. Except for one man. He spoke quietly amidst the mounting tension.

'And what about you? Do you believe he has these special powers?'

'Don't bother with the boy, Jao,' called one of the gruffer sailors. 'Can't you see he's a troublemaker?'

Jonah looked at Jao with a defiant smile.

'I only believe in me and what I do. Everyone else lets me down.'

As the last word left his mouth, there was a massive rumble of thunder. A gathering of dark grey clouds began to form, high above the lake. Soon the clouds turned black and accompanying streaks of lighting created a spectacular storm. At once, the men in the boat turned away from Jonah and began to focus on the boat, trying to protect it from the waves sweeping towards them. Many of these men were hardened fishermen used to rough crossings on the sea and the lakes, but they knew this was no ordinary storm. The rain began to lash down with a tremendous strength. The thunder bellowed loudly as waves began to crash against the sides of the boat, soaking everything they touched and threatening to swamp the boat.

Still, instead of giving way to the panic, stress, and fear around him, the Storyteller lay peacefully asleep at the front of the boat.

As if from nowhere, suddenly, from the swirls of wind and rumbles of thunder, there came a loud, eerie shriek. It surprised all the men on the boat who had never heard anything like it before. It was, however, a familiar sound to Jonah; one that he hoped never to hear again, especially without his protector by his side. He knew the deafening sound came from Theda. At that point, Jonah realised how much he needed his personal protector, but Halecim was not on the boat. He was nowhere to be seen.

Jonah started to sweat with the stress. With water from the lake dripping from his hair, he tried to prepare himself. He put his trembling hands on either side of his waist to feel for a sword but there was no weapon; nothing that he could use in battle. All he could do was try to find a firm footing on the rocking floor of the boat and use a fighting stance that Kyle had shown him in the boxing ring. Watching the sky for the arrival of his adversary, waiting for his fight to begin, Jonah stood ready.

It seemed an eternity waiting for a sight of Theda but soon the evil warrior appeared through the eye of the storm, heading straight towards his target. As Jonah looked skyward, he felt he was about to face one of the greatest battles in his life – to fight a demon. He clenched his fists and raised his hands, ready to fight. There was no strength in his arms, no bulging biceps, or rippling muscles. All he had as a weapon was courage and inner strength. Or maybe insanity, he thought.

Theda appeared to glide effortlessly towards the earth, his cloak flapping in the downward wind. As he came closer to the storm-battered boat, he drew his sword of polished steel that glistened as the sheets of lightning reflected from it. He was ready to strike. His squeal was deafening, even above the noise of the storm. The fishermen all cried out with fear, putting their hands over their ears and crouching low to get away from this evil shroud of darkness covering the boat. At their point of greatest need, they turned to the one who they knew could save them. How could he still sleep through this storm? Surely, now, they would have to wake him.

'Master,' they cried. 'Master, wake up.'

Their cries were almost muffled by the thunderous noise of the storm and crashing waves but, after a few moments, their 'Master' opened his eyes. He calmly raised himself up from his cushion and stood before the cowering men.

Jonah was still concentrating on Theda as he drew closer. 'This is it, this is the end,' he thought, as the demon approached.

Theda was now a few metres from his target, ready to strike, but before he had the chance to engage in battle, a shaft of blue-green light struck him. It was not from the lightening in the sky, however. It came from the raised right hand of the Storyteller whose hands were pointed at Theda. The demon squealed more intensely than before as the light hit him hard and sent him spiralling backwards into the storm clouds. Then the Storyteller raised his other hand and with outstretched arms shouted into the storm, 'Quiet! Be still!'

Immediately the dark, threatening clouds began to disperse, melting into a mist and revealing a clear blue sky. All was still on the surface of the lake.

The Storyteller turned to his followers and asked, 'Why are you so afraid? Do you really think that bad things will happen to you when I am with you? Do you doubt that I am able to control the wind and the rain, and fight off evil beings? Do you still have no faith in me? You have seen miraculous happenings, supernatural occurrences, unnatural events that cannot be explained and yet you still do not believe.' He then turned to Jonah and looking him straight in the eye asked, 'What will it take for you to believe?'

Jonah was about to reply when he felt a strong grip on his arm and he was whisked away towards the land by Halecim.

*** 

They arrived back in the desert, far away from the sea and any further encounter with Theda. As soon as their feet touched land, the tight grip on Jonah's hand was released and he stumbled, almost falling onto the ground again. Awkwardly, standing to his feet, he turned to face Halecim and began a barrage of questions.

'Where were you? Why did you take me away? Why did you leave me? Why did you stop me talking to the Storyteller?'

While Jonah bombarded his protector with 'whys', Halecim stood sullen as though drained of all energy. For a long while, he waited for Jonah to finish his moans and ranting. Then they both stood in complete silence, though Jonah was still seething inside. He knew that Halecim was not happy either and realised this was not the best time to continue the argument.

'I think I should go home,' said Jonah.

There was a long pause, as though Halecim did not want to answer, but then he croaked, 'Yes, I think you should. The Doorway is over there.' He pointed at a small rock formation behind Jonah's left shoulder, about twenty metres away. He stood and waited for Jonah to turn around and start walking away.

Jonah moved hesitantly but stopped in his tracks when he heard the words whispering in his ears, 'What will it take for you to believe?' He turned his head, thinking it was Halecim, but his companion had gone.

# 10

Jonah's return home through the Doorway was very quiet as he blocked all the familiar noises out of his head. Travelling at the speed of sound, through the back door of two thousand years of history, had become a normal experience for him. He was so pre-occupied with his thoughts that it never occurred to him that his homeward journey might be going wrong. The familiar ending to all his other trips had been a direct landing in his bedroom. This time he found he was deposited on the outskirts of town, about a mile away from his home. He was baffled as to why. What had changed? His mind tried hard to sift through the events of the day to try and understand this departure from the portal's normal route. Was it something to do with his adventure on the boat and the events that unfolded there?

'Maybe it wasn't Halecim's absence that allowed the fishermen to see me,' he thought to himself as he began the lengthy walk home.

Jonah was so focussed on his recent adventure that he did not fully pay attention to where he was going, until he turned down an alleyway that was controlled by the local teenage gang. This was a mistake. The gang were an unsavoury mob who thought they were the local Mafia.

Their leader, Nat, was a tall, hefty youth of fifteen stone, with ugly tattoos, piercings, shaved head, and distinctive steel-capped boots. He ruled the group of eight boys who now lined both sides of the alleyway, ready to intimidate anyone who crossed their path. Most of these boys had been permanently excluded from school and found their acceptance in Nat's gang.

'Look who's 'ere lads. If it's not the little mummy's boy from Southend Street. Feeling brave are we, coming on our turf?' said Nat as he walked up to Jonah, poking and prodding him as he spoke. He was not a natural born leader but his strength and size demanded respect from his peers.

Rumour had it that Nat's dad had run off with another woman, not long after he was born. Jonah had heard that Nat's mum had a succession of failed relationships with other men, leading to four children from four different fathers. The men had all moved on and she had been left to raise her children on her own. With a handful of youngsters, including a six-month old baby to look after, Nat's mother had not been able to cope and often could be seen outside the local off-licence with a bottle or two of Vodka. When she was drunk, Nat had to take on the role of father and look after all his younger brothers and sisters. When he had enough of his troubles at home, he took out his bitterness and anger on any boy who weaker than he was. Many a victim had suffered at the hands of Nat and his gang in this alleyway.

'Sorry, I didn't see you, I wasn't paying attention…sorry,' said Jonah, stuttering with the pressure that was on him now. He tried to turn around and walk in the opposite direction.

He did not go very far before the gang surrounded him. They searched his pockets for his mobile and laughed with disgust when they saw how old and cracked it was. Not even worth stealing.

The more uncomfortable Jonah became, the more they all laughed, especially Nat whose laughter took on a mocking tone. 'And where do you think you're going?' he said. 'You ain't got no place to go, except here with us. Loser.'

Nat's bullish disregard for another person's life was frightening and controlling. Jonah began to feel out of his depth. He had known he was in trouble as soon as he saw the gang but, at first, he thought he could negotiate his way out of the situation. That seemed unlikely now that Nat's threatening behaviour was in full flow. The situation was not good.

Jonah calculated that he had three options – to run, fight, or let himself be beaten to a pulp. He knew he could not outrun the gang and he did not want to be beaten up without a fight. The only option possible meant he was in for a rough time. Hastily, he looked around the group of teenagers trying to identify any obvious weaknesses in them. He tried to imagine himself in the boxing-ring against his arch enemy Theda, mentally preparing himself for some tricky ducking and diving. He decided to hit the biggest boy first, fearing that he would soon run out of energy and then struggle to hurt the bigger guys when he was at his weakest. Adjusting his feet into a stance that would hopefully give him the best balance, Jonah clenched his right fist tight. Quickly, he threw a punch at the boy standing to the right of Nat.

This took the gang by surprise; everyone else that they bullied usually ran away as fast as they could. No-one was expecting this weakling, this loser to fight back, especially the lad who now had Jonah's fist planted in his face. There was a brief gasp of shock as the boy stumbled backwards and dropped to the ground. Jonah's punch had hit hard. Then, as if the whistle had been blown for the start of a football match, the gang moved towards Jonah waving their arms and fists at him.

Jonah managed to give two more punches but soon his fists were caught up in the mess of arms and bodies surrounding him. It was a very quick and sudden attack, brought to an abrupt end by the loud yell of Nat's voice commanding his boys to stand down.

Three times Nat yelled out. 'Enough,' he shouted, as the crazed boys moved away from the heaped, blood-stained mess on the floor.

Only on the final word did Nat's voice reach the ears of the ravaging gang. They were all out of breath, panting as they sucked in air to calm their beating hearts, pumped high with adrenaline.

Nat looked down at Jonah who lay on the pavement. He did not look too good, but he was still breathing.

'Come on lads. Let's go,' said Nat as he walked off down the alley, followed by his subdued band of un-merry men.

There were no protectors in this urban world for Jonah. As he pushed up on his sore, bruised arms, he was not sure if his attackers were still there, but he was not going to give in easily. Straightening up, he raised his clenched hands ready to fight again. He was therefore extremely relieved to see that his assailants had already gone. Every muscle in his body was beginning to ache. He expected to have stains all over his clothes as blood dripped from his battered face, but at least one small consolation was that his shirt was not ripped.

It was time to begin the long walk home, in the opposite direction of the bully boys.

*** 

Beth shot out of her chair, heading straight towards her beaten and bruised son as he hobbled down the hall towards the kitchen. She tried to hug him close.

'Ow!' cried Jonah. 'That hurts.' He flinched and tried to push away from his mum.

'I'm sorry son, but...what's happened? Who did this to you? Why?' Beth could not stop her flow of questions coming but, as she hardly paused for breath, she didn't give Jonah a chance to provide her with any answers.

'Mum. Just stop. Let me sit down and I'll tell you everything.'

Reluctantly, Beth relaxed her grip on her son and helped him ease his way onto a kitchen chair. The fresh wounds on his body made it difficult for him to sit without letting out a squeal of pain. She took a flannel and, after soaking it in warm water, began dabbing on the cuts on Jonah's face.

Every touch of the cloth induced a flinch as Jonah tried to be brave but he struggled to keep quiet. The pain became stronger as the adrenaline in his body, produced when he was caught up in the fight, began to wear off. He suddenly felt weary.

Beth gently consoled Jonah with a hug. She was desperate to find out who had hurt him, but knew it was best not to force an explanation.

Numb with pain, they both sat in silence.

'Mum,' said Jonah after a while, 'I'm sorry.'

'Don't worry, son. I'm sure it wasn't your fault,' said Beth.

'No, I mean I'm sorry for being…well, for what I said to you before. All those horrible and hurtful words. I didn't mean them, I was angry and I …'

Beth gently put her finger on his lips. 'It's okay. I know you were upset. It's been a very difficult time for both of us. Anyway, I'm really the one to blame.'

Jonah made a motion as though to interrupt but Beth continued.

'I've spent a lot of time thinking about our lives during these last few weeks and I've started to see a counsellor. She's helped me to recognise that we are both struggling with grief and anger about things. Trouble is…these negative emotions seem to have blocked out all our memories of the good times that we used to have together.'

Jonah was surprised and not entirely convinced that his mum should see a counsellor. It was ironic that she used to be a full-time therapist herself, before the divorce. She was always helping other people through their difficult situations. Then he realised that, since that horrible day his dad left, Beth had gradually moved away from the skills she once had and never used them to help herself. He knew he was finding it helpful to talk to Halecim and listen to the words of the Storyteller so he thought, maybe, it was a good thing that his mum had someone in her life to talk to.

'Do you think we can forgive and forget everything that's happened between us and start again?' Beth suddenly asked.

Jonah nodded. It was time to put the past few months of arguments and hurts behind them. But he was wary. He thought about his dad and how he had hurt Beth. Suppose Beth wanted to forgive him and welcome him home, if the opportunity ever arose. No. That was not going to happen if Jonah had anything to do with it. Forgiving his dad was not an option for him. He had taken the place of his father in the family home and he was not going to give that position up now.

Not for anyone.

# 11

The next morning, Jonah slowly made his way down the stairs, nursing the bruised ribs on his left side. Beth was in the kitchen cooking a full-English breakfast, something she had not done for a very long time. Jonah eased his way into a chair, letting out a slight groan when his upper body made contact with the back of the chair.

Beth placed a steaming plate of sausages, beans, egg, and toast on the table in front of him.

'How are you feeling today?'

'I'm okay. A bit sore, but I'll be fine,' said Jonah.

'Shall we talk about what happened yesterday?' Beth continued.

'I don't know how that will make any difference,' Jonah said, a little uncomfortable with the subject.

'Well, I'm not going to try and sort them all out, if that's what you think!'

Jonah smiled at the thought of his mum standing face to face with Nat, telling him off for being a bully.

'I can, however, bring a different perspective on what happened and help you work out what to do next,' said Beth, warmly.

'Wow. Something good must have happened in your counselling sessions if you're starting to give advice again,' said Jonah.

'You're right son. It has been good. And it's far too long since I practiced any therapy. So why don't you tell me what happened yesterday?'

Over the next few minutes, in between mouthfuls of breakfast, Jonah relived his journey home and his difficult encounter with Nat's gang – not mentioning why he was walking home from the other side of town in the first place.

'I don't know what gives them the right to think they own the alleyway, dictating who can and can't pass,' he said.

'I think the reason they feel they have the right to rule is because no one ever challenges them,' said Beth. 'They probably feel powerful when they are together, but I suspect the reason for this is because they feel powerless in their family lives.'

'What do you mean, Mum?'

'I know this sounds strange coming from me but I used to specialise in helping couples work out difficult family relationships.'

Jonah was confused. How could Beth have done that when she had so many problems at home with his dad?

'Yes, I know what you're thinking,' Beth continued, before Jonah had a chance to speak. 'When you work in a job that consumes all your mental and emotional energy, you very often forget to apply the same principles to your home life. It often suffers.' Beth paused. 'A relationship works best when two people treat each other with respect and support each other's growth. But when a relationship is based on power, especially an abuse of power, then one person tends to dominate the other. When a parent uses power over their child, instead of loving and supporting them, the child copies this behaviour in other relationships. They try and find ways to take control and abuse any power they gain.'

Jonah wondered where his mother was going with this argument. Then she said something that began to make sense.

'I suspect that the boys who hurt you need to threaten other people because at home they feel weak and misunderstood. They've lost their belief in family life and built strong walls around their hearts to stop any pain getting in - a bit like we both have, over the past three years.'

'And I just thought they were bullies because they chose to be,' said Jonah.

He had finished his breakfast now but still sat at the kitchen table, contemplating what his mother had said. Until now, he had thought the bullies were horrible people but now he began to feel a little bit sorry for them. At least, even though his dad had left home, his mum had never tried to control him. As he considered his relationship with Beth, he realised that some of his recent behaviour towards her had been aggressive, perhaps even abusive.

He raised his head towards his mum and she ever so slightly smiled at him. He wondered if she had guessed what had just gone through his mind.

***

Although there were aches and pains all over Jonah's body, he needed to be in a place where he felt safe and where he could think about his life, without being disturbed. He packed his bag with a pair of jogging bottoms, a vest, towel, shower gel, deodorant, and his comb - all the essentials for a good workout at the gym. In the world through the Doorway, Halecim was his protector, but in the reality of this world, Kyle was his mentor. The gym was a source of strength and he was eager to train again. He said goodbye to his mum before he left, for the first time in ages, and closed the door behind him.

He walked towards the gym, past the park where he had seen his dad and towards Nat's alleyway. He stood at the entrance to the passage where the day before he had suffered at the hands of the local mob and stared down the pathway. As he was about to move, he noticed someone at the other end of the alleyway who had also stopped and was looking in his direction. It was Nat. Jonah stared at him, calmly. He wasn't fearful anymore; why should he be? Compared to having the evil warrior-demon Theda trying to kill him, this was nothing. This lonely figure of a boy whom, overnight, Jonah had come to pity, was all alone and not a threat anymore.

Nat, however, seemed quite uncomfortable seeing Jonah again, so soon after his beating. Other victims had never reacted this way before. The more that Jonah stood calm and silent, the more Nat looked twitchy and stressed. It seriously unnerved him. He quickly moved on.

***

Jonah arrived at the gym, eagerly pushing the doors open to get inside. He looked around the room, his gaze searching for the man in the far corner who was teaching a young lad how to skip. Passing several boys and men, training with punch bags and weights or sparring together, Jonah made his way to the changing rooms. He speedily prepared himself for what he thought might be a gruelling session.

Returning to the main floor of the gym, Jonah made his way over to the skipping area,

'Hi Kyle, I need your help today. If you're free,' he said, respectfully.

'Hi Jonah. No problem. Start on the bike for ten minutes and then we'll get you working.'

Jonah spent the next two hours pushing his body through the pain barrier and sweating uncontrollably. He had forgotten about his wounds from yesterday's beatings. They were a distant memory compared to the strain that he was putting his body through now.

'I think that's enough for today Jonah,' said Kyle.

'No, I want to do more,' said Jonah, stubbornly.

'I said, that's enough for today,' Kyle repeated, firmly. Following a short pause, he continued, 'Get yourself changed, and we'll have a chat in the café if you're up for it.'

Jonah realised he shouldn't push against Kyle so he agreed and left the gym for the showers.

*** 

The entrance of the community centre had several white plastic tables and chairs scattered to the left of the entrance. The reception desk doubled up as a servery for buying refreshments and hot and cold snacks. Recently, the council had begun promoting healthy living and convinced the café to sell fresh fruit and energy shakes. Kyle had already purchased two shakes, ready for Jonah when he arrived. Putting his kit bag on one of the spare plastic chairs, Jonah sagged into the seat opposite Kyle. As he sat, he clenched his face in a grimace as the pain wrenched from his ribs sent shockwaves up his body. It wasn't from the strenuous workout but from his battle with Nat's gang the day before.

'Thanks for the drink, and 'erm, sorry for my little outburst earlier,' Jonah said, reaching for his glass and beginning to sip the energy shake.

Kyle leaned forward, staring at the bruises on his face. 'Jonah, what's happening in your life?'

Jonah stopped slurping his drink and slowly sat back in his chair. What could he say?

'It's a long story and I don't think you'd believe me anyway.'

Although Jonah wanted to share his recent experiences with Kyle, he knew that tales of flying back in time and fighting evil demons was too much for anyone to believe.

'Why don't you try me?' said Kyle, opening his hands as though he was about to catch a ball.

Jonah paused for thought before deciding where to start. He thought it was probably best to begin with the things that happened in this world, so he started to explain why his ribs were hurting,

'I ran into some of the boys from the estate yesterday and took a bit of a pasting.'

Instantly, Kyle stood up, almost knocking both drinks over as the unstable plastic table shook beneath them.

'What did I say?' said Jonah. 'Where are you going?' He was worried he had said something to upset Kyle.

'Nat and his boys used to train here but they only wanted to use what they learned to hurt others,' said Kyle, looking angry. 'I saw them last week and told them that if I found out they were intimidating anyone else, they'd have me to deal with.'

'Hang on, you can't go and fight my battles for me,' said Jonah, hastily. 'And anyway, I threw the first punch.'

'What? Why?' Kyle asked, in obvious disbelief.

'They tried to intimidate me and crowded round me and threatened me. I knew the one thing they wouldn't expect from a weakling like me was a fight, so I lashed out and got three of them first.'

Jonah wasn't sure whether grinning was appropriate, as Kyle was so cross, but he couldn't help himself.

Kyle joined in with the smile for a moment, and then sat down again. 'Well, this certainly wasn't what I was expecting to hear,' he said.

Jonah thought he should try to offer some further explanation. 'I have other battles going on in my life too. You taught me that I need to fight from within…to find strength, courage and belief in myself. So, on this occasion, I knew I couldn't outrun them or talk my way out of it. All I could do was try and surprise them with a couple of punches so that, hopefully, they'd all be in shock and I could slip away. I was right about the surprise - but it seemed to turn them into a pack of animals. All except Nat. He just watched for a while before calling the dogs off.'

Kyle looked intrigued at these revelations. 'What about the other battles you mentioned?' he asked.

'Well, um, you see…my dad left me and mum three years ago. He ran off with another woman. It broke my mum's heart and it made me very angry that he thought more about himself than about us. And it's been getting harder and harder for mum and me to live together. We're constantly arguing and fighting. I said some really bad things to mum a couple of weeks ago and we didn't speak to each other for days. After I arrived home from yesterday's beating, though, we found the time and space to say sorry. So, we've agreed to start again.'

'Then that's good, isn't it?' said Kyle. 'Why is it still a battle?'

'After three years of being away, suddenly my dad turned up in the park this week. No letters, no text, no warning – nothing. He just showed up and started talking to me. He must have been following me. I didn't have a chance to think, I was so angry about the pain he'd caused. I flew off the handle, said some horrible things, and sent him away.'

'Do you regret that?'

'No. I'm just concerned that he'll try to worm his way back into my mum's life. He looked a mess so I'm guessing he must have been dumped by his girlfriend and he's come crawling back thinking we'll accept him with open arms.'

Jonah paused. He really didn't know whether to say the next few words or whether to end this informal 'counselling' session there. He wished he could hold his tongue but, although his head was telling him to keep his mouth shut, he burst out with words he instantly regretted.

'And there is something evil coming after me.'

Kyle looked concerned. 'Evil, eh? Tell me more.'

Jonah was not sure how much he should reveal so he kept silent.

'Look,' said Kyle, after a while. 'I have to admit I don't really know how to offer help or advice about the absent father thing. But I do know how to fight. And fighting evil…now, that's a whole, different story. I've travelled around the world's boxing arenas and seen many strange wonders and experiences that can't be easily explained. I've become more and more convinced that there is a supernatural world.'

'Do you believe in good and evil?'

'Yes,' said Kyle.

Jonah lowered his voice. 'Do you believe in demons?'

Kyle hesitated and then replied, almost cagily, 'I believe there is a supernatural world, yes. I believe there's a fight going on between good and evil spirits. I've had many conversations with all sorts of people around the world and I think there is evidence that angels and demons exist. What do you believe, Jonah?'

Those last five words triggered an echo of the same question fired at Jonah before - from the Storyteller, from Halecim and from Beth. The last words he remembered in Halecim's world were, 'What will it take for you to believe?'

Jonah thought carefully about his answer. 'I believe both good and evil exists, sure, and I guess I believe in a greater being that made them. Like you, I believe there is another world where good and evil spirits battle, but I think they fight to either protect or hurt humans. I'm not convinced about angels but I certainly know demons exist.'

'I once had a fight in the USA,' Kyle said 'where I came across an old Native American man who I spent a lot of time with. We used to sit around an open fire, smoke a peace pipe - well he smoked and I passively inhaled - and he would tell me stories of old legends from his tribe. One that I always remember was from an old Cherokee, teaching his grandson about life. It went like this, "There is a terrible fight going on inside me, between two wolves. One wolf is evil - he is anger, envy, greed, arrogance, self-pity, guilt, lies, and all that is bad. The other wolf is good - he is joy, peace, love, hope, humility, kindness, truth, compassion, and faith. The same fight is going on inside everyone." The grandson thought about it for a minute and then asked, "Which wolf will win, Grandfather?" The old Cherokee simply replied, "The one we feed."

Kyle was silent for a moment, before looking at Jonah intently. 'Do you think you might be feeding your demons?'

Jonah shrugged. He was not convinced by the story. He had already heard tales like this from the Storyteller. He did not believe they had any personal relevance to his own life. 'I don't really think that I have to feed or starve anyone to win this fight, except me. And right now, I'm starving.' Then he stood up quickly, made his apologies, and started to leave. As he did, he heard Kyle's voice behind him.

'It sounds to me like the evil is being fed more…and it's winning.'

Jonah turned his head away from Kyle and walked through the open door.

# 12

It was a clear, cloudless evening with millions of stars shining brightly in the sky, as far as the eye could see. The radiance from those stars travelled light-years through space to reach the earth and, on this night, they provided a clear view for anyone taking an evening stroll. The moon shone too, amidst the twinkling stars, making the night-time scene a magical sight.

It was therefore a strange anomaly to see a cloud-like shadow smother the tattered bench in the park with thick black smoke. It seemed to appear from nowhere and rested over the exact spot that Jonah's father had waited for him a few days earlier. Could it be a sign that the Doorway had become unstable? Not only had it misplaced Jonah's last exit point, it had started to lose control of who came through its entrance and was becoming increasingly fragile as a secure portal. It seemed that Jonah's two worlds were about to collide.

\*\*\*

Beth opened the front door and walked into the hall. She smelt an unusual aroma. As far back as she could remember she had not walked into her own home to be greeted by the lovely smell of someone else's cooking. At first, she thought she had left the cooker on since the morning. Then, as she took her coat off and walked towards the kitchen, she was surprised to see Jonah standing there. He was frantically stirring the vegetables in the wok so that they didn't stick to the bottom of the pan. The kitchen looked like a bomb had recently exploded in it. Dirty glass bowls and pans were piled up in the sink, spilling out onto the draining board. Liquids of all sorts had been spilt on the worktops, dripping down the cupboard doors onto the floor. Normally, Beth would be furious, shouting at the mess Jonah had made. Instead, she was thrilled that her son had taken the time to cook for her. She stood in the entrance to the kitchen, leant against the door frame, and smiled.

'Ah, Mum, you're home early. I was hoping to have this all ready for you when you got here,' said Jonah quickly, whilst balancing several cooking implements.

'It looks like you could do with some help. I'd love to join in, if you want me to.'

'Course you can, Mum, you don't need to ask,' said Jonah with a sigh of relief at the offer of help.

'Oh, but I do need to ask. I can't just barge in and take over, especially if you planned to do it all yourself.'

'But you know how to get this right. It's better than me burning it!' said Jonah, looking at the frazzled mess in the pan.

'Just because I can, doesn't mean that I should. It's nice that you want me to, but I still need to ask. Remember how a good relationship works best?'

Beth had returned from another therapy session and was still trying to psychoanalyse every situation. Jonah, on the other hand, wanted to cook food that they could eat, not throw in the bin.

'Mum, come on in and try and salvage this mess, please.'

For the first time in ages, Jonah was glad to have his mum next to him.

Later, they enjoyed a lovely meal together, finishing with a chocolate cheesecake from the local shop. They smiled and joked about the mess, both revived by the happiness that had been absent from their home for a very long time.

'I'll wash. You dry,' said Beth afterwards.

They began stacking the plates and dishes together as they cleared the table. Although these happy moments were good for them both, it didn't take long before Jonah began worrying about the past few days and the difficulties he had faced. He was confronted by many challenges and, as he reflected on this mixture of new emotions, he became very quiet.

'Are you okay?' asked Beth, recognising the sudden change in her son.

Jonah snapped out of his dream-world when he heard his mum's voice. 'Yeah, I'm okay. There are some things we need to talk about but I don't want to spoil this evening, so it can wait until tomorrow.'

'Are you sure? I don't mind talking now,' said Beth.

'No, it can wait. What about sitting in front of the television with some popcorn, like we used to?'

'Sounds good to me,' said Beth.

***

A clear, cloudless sky meant only one thing: it was a cold evening for those who stood around the alleyways on the estate. Jumping up and down, running on the spot, and play-fighting filled the evening as Nat's gang attempted to keep warm. There was nothing constructive to do whilst hanging around these concrete passages so the teenage boys were forced to create their own entertainment. Much of their time was spent playing games of football with empty drink cans.

Occasionally, they would try to impress the teenage girls from the estate with displays of macho manliness and strength, tensing their biceps so hard that the blood rushed to their faces and turned their skin colour three shades darker. As the girls walked past, they would just laugh and keep on moving. However, on the rare occasion that a vulnerable person, a potential victim, accidently strayed into their path, the boys became very excited and prepared themselves for their favourite form of entertainment – violence.

A clear, bright, and crisp evening was one of those nights the teenagers looked forward to the most.

On this same night, a lonely twelve-year old boy approaching the gang thought that this was the time to do something brave, to stop feeling like a coward. Colin had often been the focus of other children's jokes. He was smaller and weaker than the rest of the lads; his glasses, ginger hair, acne, and old ripped clothes gave others plenty of excuses to attack and bully him. Tonight, however, Colin believed that, if he stood up straight and walked confidently through the group, he could outsmart and even out-run the gang who ruled the local streets. This new self-belief was consuming his thoughts when he turned into the alleyway and walked towards the gang. He felt invincible. For a few seconds, anyway.

Colin had expected the taunting and verbal abuse to come thick and fast, he could cope with that, but he began to lose confidence when some larger boys began to circle him, shoving him from one to another. It began to feel dangerous.

As some of the group crowded around Colin, others sat on a wall, just watching, next to Nat who was unusually quiet.

It was all a bit of fun, some light entertainment to warm the lads up on a cold evening. However, the last time the gang were standing here was when they encountered Jonah. One of the boys, Kane, began thinking about that time when Jonah unexpectedly lashed out and hit one of his mates. He didn't want anything like this to happen again and decided he needed to stop any potential threat by attacking first. He clenched his fist, raised his arm, and directed it at Colin's right cheek with such force that he knocked his glasses right off his face. Colin tumbled to the ground in shock.

Although the gathering crowd of boys were used to beating up the vulnerable, they had not expected such an early outburst of violence to come from one of their crew. When Kane lashed out, in traditional mob style they took it as a sign that it was okay to move in for the kill. One by one, they joined in the onslaught of their victim.

As Colin lay on the ground, he began to cry with the extreme pain throbbing in his face and down the back of his neck. His pitiful cries and shrieks suddenly became too much for Nat to bear and, before long, he shouted for order amongst his gang. At the sound of their leader's voice, Kane and the rest of Nat's followers stopped and stared at him, confused and bewildered. They could not understand why he was trying to stop their fun.

'What's going on Nat?' said Dan, his irritation close to the surface. As Nat's deputy he was the only one who ever dared challenge his leadership.

Nat stared at the group in angry silence. He moved swiftly towards Colin, carefully helped him up to his feet and whispered in his ear, 'Run.'

As Colin limped away as fast as he could, Dan stared at Nat in disbelief. He was not impressed that his evening's entertainment had been spoiled. He asked again, this time with anger in his voice, 'What's going on?'

Nat's response was completely out of character. 'This has gone too far. It's not right.'

Dan could not believe what he was hearing. 'Gone soft on us Nat, 'ave we? Something turned you into one of them 'as it?' he said, with a sarcastic tone and mocking grin.

With incredible speed, Nat whipped a flick knife from a pocket in the back of his trousers and brought it up directly underneath Dan's chin. When Dan felt the point of the blade touch his skin, he immediately lost his courage and stopped his short-lived act of defiance. Everyone knew Nat was not afraid to use his knife; he'd done so several times before.

'You may be my best mate Dan but remember your place,' Nat said in a quiet, deep voice, his words hissing through gritted teeth. He stared with piercing eyes at Dan, forcing him to close his eyes. Slowly he lowered the knife several millimetres away from Dan's chin, hooked his right leg around his right ankle and pushed him backwards, causing Dan to fall over the outstretched leg and collapse onto the ground.

The other lads, especially Kane, looked on in shock. No one spoke as Nat silently walked away, leaving them staring at him from the distance.

# 13

The sun shone brightly through the thin curtains that hung in the smaller of the two bedrooms in Jonah's house. The rays of brilliant white and yellow and the warmth from the sun, reflecting on the window pane, warmed Jonah's face and woke him from a deep sleep. Surprised, he shot out of bed thinking that the Doorway was about to arrive. He had become very used to sudden shafts of light appearing through his bedroom window, revealing the entrance to his secret world, but he usually had some control over when that came. He was usually ready and waiting. This time, however, was different. He wondered if the Doorway needed some maintenance, if it was possibly faulty and in need of some repair. He wasn't particularly ready at that moment to go back and meet Halecim again, especially as they had parted under difficult circumstances the last time, but Jonah thought he had better get dressed and be prepared, just in case.

The familiar rays of light piercing through the window and patterning the opposite wall appeared more intense than he had ever seen them before. The breeze that followed the light quickly turned into a raging wind, swirling and crashing around his bedroom. The blinding light burned an image onto the wall. There wasn't even time for Jonah to brush his teeth before the Doorway was ready to be opened. He felt exceptionally cautious and wary about being summoned by the door so early in the day, but everything else in his life was crazy now so he was ready for the challenge.

'What the hell, let's give it a go.'

He waited to be lifted from the floor and taken effortlessly through the entrance to the portal, not knowing if the normal routine would be changing too. After a few minutes, it was clear that the journey was taking a different route from usual; there was no passing of local landmarks, or a parade through points in history where famous people and places whizzed by. This time it was just Jonah, alone in the portal. The atmosphere seemed darker than usual; the shooting shafts of light were not so bright or sparkly, nothing was white anymore - more of a muddy grey, and it felt cold in the portal. There was a sinister sense of something ominous in the air and it sent chills through Jonah's body. He was relieved to see the exit approaching. Even though he knew he was about to confront his protector again, it had to be better than the unsettling nature of his journey so far.

As usual, Halecim was waiting for him on the other side, but there were no smiles or hugs of welcome this time. Before Jonah's body had even left the Doorway, Halecim had grabbed his right arm and dragged him vigorously and speedily away from the exit. He did not speak but moved swiftly, causing Jonah to catch his left leg in the door and having to scrape it free as the portal closed behind him. They were travelling faster than usual; the wind blew cold against his un-brushed teeth and Jonah felt the full force of the wind on his cheeks. He was very nervous about how fast things were changing and worried about what was going to happen when they reached their destination.

A dark cave, deep in the mountains, was their usual hiding place from Theda but, today, they headed towards a town on the edge of a large lake. Jonah recalled the image of this lake from his last adventure with Halecim. Shivers went down his spine as he remembered how he was left alone and his enemy Theda tried to attack him on the fishing boat in the storm. He managed a quick glance to check the sky. It was a clear blue. Thank goodness, not a cloud in sight.

They arrived at the edge of the town where no-one could see them and stood within hearing distance of a large crowd that had gathered on the main street. Halecim gently let go of Jonah's arm, scanning the area carefully to make sure they had not been followed. Jonah had so many questions but he was very cautious about how to start the conversation. He did not want to upset Halecim again or have an early exit back to the darkening Doorway.

'Hello Halecim, how are you?' he said, as politely as he could.

'Hello Jonah. I wasn't sure if you were brave enough to come back.'

'Why? Because I upset you and the Storyteller?'

Halecim smiled at this suggestion. 'You didn't upset us. I was talking about the rise of Vilde and the changing atmosphere around us.'

'Yes, I've noticed that too, lots of changes, but not just here,' said Jonah, some stress-lines on his face revealing his deep anxiety.

'What do you mean?'

'Strange things are happening at home. The last time I left through the Doorway, I ended up a mile away from my house. It was different on the way here too. Darker, colder, intimidating.' Jonah shivered as he remembered his journey.

Halecim looked very concerned. 'I didn't realise this could happen...that it could get this bad.'

'What could get so bad, Halecim?'

'The last time you were here, Theda came to attack you and the men in the boats saw him. They also saw you. The evil warrior has seen this as a great opportunity to attack you and many others, including my Master.'

'I thought he was only interested in me?' said Jonah

'Don't think you are that unique, young man. He wants as many souls as he can get. But you do have a special part to play. You have an important role in making history,' said Halecim.

Jonah stood up straight, smiling with pride that he some sort of influence. This pleasure didn't last long as Halecim continued to explain that the current state of affairs was not good and that Jonah was partly to blame for the problems that they were now encountering.

Halecim almost whispered these words as though he was not supposed to be sharing this information with Jonah: 'You need to understand that Vilde and his followers, including Theda, thrive on evil, on the dark and sinister side of life. To do this they feed on unbelief, and you have been giving them a banquet. They grow stronger each day as you, and many other humans in this world, choose not to believe in the Storyteller or in what he does. Your disbelief has caused a crack in time that is allowing a new type of evil to pass through.'

'Oh, believe me, Halecim...there is already plenty of evil where I come from. It doesn't need me to create a passage for it to travel anywhere.'

'You do this every time,' said Halecim, once again frustrated with Jonah. 'You ignore the seriousness of what I have just told you and focus on something else that you can make light of. Or a sarcastic comment. Anyway, I've said enough. You're supposed to be working this out for yourself. But be careful. Other people may be able to see you now and Theda may not attack alone next time.'

'Is that why we're here, in this public place, and not hiding in a cave?' said Jonah.

'No, we are here because this is where the Storyteller is, and that makes this the safest place on earth.' Halecim then produced, as if from nowhere, a long dirty-white garment. It looked as if it was made from one strip of material, full length with three-quarter length sleeves.

Jonah immediately recognised it as the same fashion everyone else in the town was wearing. 'You've got to be joking,' he said.

Ignoring him, Halecim threw him the garment and Jonah reluctantly put it on. It wasn't a bad look, he thought - a white dress over his t-shirt and jeans with his trainers peeping out at the hemline. Halecim changed his outer clothing too, so that he looked more like an ordinary man, only taller and heftier.

They began to walk into town, following the noise of the crowd. Halecim was walking quickly, as if he was in a hurry. Jonah was struggling to keep up with him, especially as he kept tripping over the hem of his tunic. They eventually turned off the side-street into a very crowded main thoroughfare, with hundreds of people (including children) squashing, pushing, and shoving each other out of the way. Each person tried to move in front of the next, trying to get closer to the front of the queue and see what was causing all the commotion.

Although Halecim appeared like an ordinary man, he was still far taller than anyone else was, and strong enough to move people out of the way with the gentlest of pushes. Jonah kept close behind him, tucked in tight to his shadow, as they made their way through the hustle and bustle of the crowd. The excited talking and laughing suddenly dwindled, drowned out by shocking cries of pain and grief. The wailing of women, and shouts of despair from several people close to Jonah, began to crescendo. The mood of the crowd had changed and only the foreigner in the crowd struggled to grasp what was happening.

'Halecim, Halecim, what's that noise...what's going on?' Jonah was tugging at his protector's clothes, trying to get his attention through the noise.

Halecim led Jonah to an alleyway, away from the crowd but close enough to the action to see what was happening. 'The Storyteller is on his way to the house where a young girl is very poorly. It looks like the servants of the girl's father have come to tell him not to bother. She must already be dead.'

'Oh no, that's terrible.' Jonah did not know what else to say at first but, after a while, asked, 'Why didn't they go to a doctor?'

Halecim gave Jonah a look of frustration. 'Because the girl's father believed the Storyteller could help her. He asked him to go and put his hands on her and make her better. That is where he was heading, but his journey was delayed because another person needed his help too.'

Although so much had happened recently, Jonah still didn't understand who the Storyteller was, or why he could heal all these people. 'So, what happens now?' He thought he should know the answer to this but was still completely baffled and too impatient to wait and see.

Halecim hushed him.

Together, they watched the Storyteller touch the shoulder of the girl's father to offer some comfort. With compassion in his eyes, he simply said, 'Don't be afraid. Just believe.'

The man looked back at the Storyteller with an expression that suggested he trusted this man and all would be well.

Jonah was amazed at how five words could induce such a response. He remembered the Storyteller saying the same words to him, on the boat, but it did not affect him in the same way. Why, he wondered? Was it because he was full of anger but this man was full of pain? Was it because this man already believed and Jonah did not?

The Storyteller did not want the crowds to follow him anymore. He only wanted to take three of his friends, and the girl's father, into the house where the girl lay. He commanded his other companions to disperse the crowds and make sure no-one followed them.

Keeping out of sight, Halecim led Jonah swiftly between the houses and followed the small group from a distance. As they drew closer to the home of the young girl, they heard crying and wailing.

Grief had overtaken the family since the girl had already died earlier. The Storyteller was not welcomed with happiness. Instead, the mourners were resentful and blamed him for the girl's death. The Storyteller did not seem surprised by this, or troubled by the poor reception they gave him, but simply walked past them, followed by the girl's father, and went into the house. As he passed, he turned and said, 'Why are you all making such a noise? She is not dead, but only sleeping.'

The people outside stopped their squealing and crying and gave an outburst of mocking laughter at such outrageous claims.

Jonah thought that he would have been exceptionally angry if they had laughed at him like that. However, the Storyteller ignored his mockers, remaining calm and peaceful and entered the house.

Halecim somehow managed to smuggle Jonah with him into the bedroom where the little girl lay. As the Storyteller entered the room, he firmly announced the need for everyone to leave. The room cleared exceptionally quickly, but the girl's mum and dad, and the Storyteller's three friends, were permitted to stay. Halecim and Jonah were already hidden behind a cupboard, peering from behind their camouflage to witness the action. The girl lay on her bed, peaceful and still, not moving at all. There was no breathing in her body, no blink of her eyelids. The Storyteller had told the crowd she was sleeping but she looked dead to everyone else in the room, including Jonah.

Nobody said a word as everyone watched and waited.

The Storyteller reached down towards the girl and gently took her hand, clasping it in his. Looking directly at her, he said in a quiet, comforting voice, 'Little girl, wake up.'

To everyone's amazement, the girl immediately opened her eyes, stood to her feet, and walked around the room to hug her parents. They looked at her in wonder.

'She is hungry, prepare some food,' said the Storyteller. 'And listen very carefully…do not, for any reason, tell people outside this room what has happened. What you have seen stays in this room, do you understand?' His tone was now very strict, like a headmaster warning his pupils not to be disobedient. He obviously did not want other people to know what had happened in that room.

Jonah did not intend to tell anyone in the crowd of people who were starting to gather outside. He did not quite understand what had just happened anyway. Had she just been asleep, or was this now a cover-up so that the people who saw the girl alive would believe the Storyteller's earlier statement? Jonah was confused. If what he saw was real, did this man really have power and authority over death itself − without any medicine, defibrillators, or medical procedures? Could he heal with just a simple, whispered command?

The commotion and excitement in the room, as friends and relatives watched the girl walking around the house, was enough of a diversion for Halecim and Jonah to slip out through the back door of the house, unnoticed. They headed in the opposite direction of the Storyteller, who had also taken his leave and walked away from the house with his friends.

It was a short journey towards the edge of the town, but one they spent in silence, as both Halecim and Jonah were deep in thought. They reached the seashore and walked slowly along the beach. Up until this point, Jonah had usually been four paces behind Halecim's massive strides. Now, he had a chance to catch up and continue to walk alongside him.

'Can I ask why we are not with the Storyteller when, two hours ago, you said it was the safest place to be?' said Jonah.

'Because, surprisingly, you are starting to believe.'

'What do you mean?'

'Theda, our evil warrior was feeding off your unbelief.'

'Yes, you've already told me that,' said Jonah, feeling impatient again.

'Two hours ago, he was at his strongest. Then the safest place to be was with the one whom he has no authority over – the Storyteller.'

'So, what has changed in the past two hours?' said Jonah. 'What has enabled us to walk along this quiet beach instead of hiding or running for our lives?'

'You, Jonah. You.'

Jonah was not expecting that. He grew very quiet as he tried to sift through all the experiences he had witnessed recently and his earlier adventures in this strange land. What did Halecim mean? After a long pause, the penny seemed to drop. 'Okay. I believe that the girl was already dead and that the Storyteller brought her back to life.'

Halecim tried to disguise the smile on his face. This was the first time that Jonah had expressed any sign of belief.

'But how did he do it?'

'That's not a bad question, Jonah…the best you've asked so far. You can probably answer that one yourself, if you think about it a bit deeper. There is another question, a more important one you need to be asking me now.'

'Things are never easy and straightforward with you,' Jonah said in frustration. He still had not had a direct reply, even though it was, apparently, his best-ever question.

'Well, go through everything you have learned already.' Halecim was trying to give as much help as he could, probably too much help, but he wanted Jonah to get to grips with the facts quicker than he usually did.

Jonah was not the greatest of thinkers; he was more of a practical person. If he had the chance to sit and think, his mind would generally wonder into fantasies about winning the lottery, being a spy, or just drifting into space. Any thinking that involved analysis was generally beyond his capabilities. Still, he knew he had to try.

Halecim took great delight watching Jonah strain to think – his raised eyebrows, frowns galore, and twitching lips. All the effort he was putting in would soon surely resolve the many questions he had.

'I can't do this,' Jonah eventually said in frustration.

'Do what?' replied Halecim.

'Think!' cried Jonah, which sent his oversized friend into a fit of laughter.

'Stop making fun of me, it's not nice.' Jonah became very defensive and sat on the floor in a huff, bending his head into an almost foetal position where he felt safe.

Halecim stopped laughing aloud, but he could not suppress a smile.

\*\*\*

Theda knelt before his master, concerned that he would be punished for failing to kill his target. This was no ordinary place; it was freezing cold but burning hot at the same time. The blue ice covering the walls and ceiling glimmered through the blazing flames that randomly appeared everywhere, then disappeared as quickly as they came. Smoking embers tumbled to the ground before being fanned back upwards with the next burst of flames. However hot it became, the ice never melted. This unnatural mix of elements created constant pain for those who were trapped in this dark place. There was no goodness, happiness, or beauty. It was dangerous, dark, and disturbing.

In charge of the demonic warriors was Vilde, a vile-looking beast, disfigured by living for thousands of years in this hell-hole. He constantly fed on wicked souls and the evil deeds of humanity. Although he was horrible to look at, his features had a vague reminiscence to Halecim's; not that they looked anything like each other now. He remembered, many centuries ago, they had come from the same mould but now Vilde had burnt off his wings and instead his muscular arms were black and red, mutilated by the scars of centuries of fighting.

Now, Vilde's palace was not made of gold or jewels. It was not spectacular or grand; in fact, there were no carved walls or ceilings, balconies or columns, as there had been, when he shared a palace with Halecim. Now he dwelt amongst fire, ice, and darkness.

Theda knelt on his right knee, with his arms folded and his head bowed low. He was still, very still, as he waited in trepidation to see how his master was going to react.

Vilde, over ten feet tall, with flames of fire burning from his hands and feet, towered over the gaunt, cloaked warrior who knelt before him. The tremendous heat from the fire, blending with the icy air that was also present, caused steam to rise from his shoulders and head. Although his face was disfigured, his expression of anger at Theda's failure was clear. His cheek (only one of these was visible, as the other had been crushed into his face) began to bubble, and his burnt skin glowed, revealing the throbbing black veins that lay beneath. Sweat poured down his face and dripped onto the warrior at his feet. Grunts, groans, and other disturbing noises seeped from the back of his throat, followed by a bellow of rage that started from deep within his stomach and belched from his widely stretched mouth. 'Why is he still alive?' he shouted.

'Forgive me, my Lord. Whenever I get close to him, Halecim appears,' said Theda. Although he never visibly showed fear, his master scared the life out of him.

'What's Halecim doing, looking after that boy?' Vilde's voice grew louder.

'I don't know my lord, but he's always there.'

'Hmm. The boy must be more valuable than I thought. Our great Enemy wouldn't put his best protector in charge of such a weak human if he didn't think it was important.'

Vilde's rage had turned to curiosity. He began pacing around the floor, circling Theda as he contemplated this new information.

'My lord, how can I beat Halecim?' Theda was concerned that Vilde might confuse his question with weakness rather than giving him a combat strategy.

'Halecim and I were friends once…created as equals,' said Vilde. 'I spent much time trying to convince him to join me, but he refused. He is committed to protecting all that is good. He is happy to serve rather than to be served…the fool.'

Vilde thought back to times long past. Forgetting Theda, he became absorbed in thoughts of what could have been, if Halecim had joined his forces. It was so long ago that he had forgotten the feelings of their original friendship. There was nothing good left in Vilde now, not since his attempt to overthrow his own Creator and rule the universe. His selfish greed and desire for power had caused him to forget the reason why he had been created – to care and nurture the world, not to destroy it. He couldn't create anything, except pain and misery. He only cared about power and revenge. The mention of Halecim and the memories it brought about his past made Vilde angrier than anything that was happening in the present.

This pleased Theda.

'Halecim's weakness is caring – showing concern for those stupid humans,' said Vilde. 'He does not have permission to show himself in this modern world but, if you find the woman who gave birth to this child, you will be able to trap the boy.'

'Yes, my lord.'

Theda knew he had only narrowly escaped punishment for his failed attempt to kill Jonah. He slowly moved backwards away from his master, until he was far enough away to stand, and quickly turned around. He moved through a line of warriors waiting on guard, who bowed their heads in respect and resumed their stance when he had passed.

# 14

Jonah lay on his bed, deep in thought. He was still struggling to figure everything out. There was a lot of information for him to sift through before he could put all the pieces of the puzzle together. Although he was starting to get a headache, he continued, in his mind, to put the previous events in some sort of order and examine the evidence for anything of interest. After only a short while, he gave up and closed his eyes. Maybe lying on the bed, with his head on his soft, fluffy pillow, trying to think, was not the best method for success! A gentle knock on his door stopped him from drifting into a deep sleep.

'Yeah?' Jonah mumbled, out of the corner of his mouth.

'It's only me. Can I come in?' replied his mum. Listening intently for an answer, with her right ear close to the door, she interpreted her son's second grunt as a 'yes' and pushed the door open.

Apart from the sweaty gym clothes that lay on the floor, Jonah's bedroom was surprisingly tidy, probably because he didn't spend that much time in it.

'As it's Saturday, I just wondered if you fancied a treat for lunch.'

'Is it that time already? I need to go to the gym first, but is it okay if you meet me outside the community centre at about 2 o'clock? Then we can eat?'

'Yes, that's fine, Jonah. It'll be nice,' said Beth, smiling.

'Yes, Mum. It will be.'

It had been a very long time since they shared a happy outing together. Family treats used to happen regularly when Jonah's dad was around, but that was in the distant past. It was hard to believe that so much had changed since then, and now they were starting to change for the better. Jonah and his mother were beginning to enjoy being together again. It felt as if they were in a positive place in their relationship.

Beth left the room and Jonah packed his bag, ready for the gym.

***

It was a good training session. Jonah felt relaxed, light on his feet, and worked hard, stretching his muscles to help the blood pump faster. He started his workout on the exercise bikes for ten minutes, and then the running machine for twenty minutes. Although he found these exercises boring, compared to lifting weights and hitting the punch bag, he knew he had to improve his overall fitness and speed - in case he had to run from Theda, rather than stand and fight. He moved onto the freestanding weights to build muscle in his arms, chest, back, and shoulders. He would need all the help he could muster to swing a heavy sword around his head.

Jonah was beginning to feel happy about his physique, especially when he looked in the full-length mirrors and noticed that his body had become more toned. Checking the room to see that no-one was looking in his direction, he went for a full bodybuilder's pose, flexing his muscles and straining them hard to make them seem bigger. He stopped and suddenly felt the blood rushing through his cheeks, turning red with embarrassment.

'Nice pose, Jonah,' said Kyle, behind him.

Jonah didn't know whether to hide or run away. He quietly said 'thank you' and made his way over to the punch bag, putting protective tape on his hands along the way.

'Let me hold the bag for you,' said Kyle, conscious of Jonah's embarrassment.

'Okay, thanks,' said Jonah, unable to look Kyle in the eyes.

'So, how's it all going?' Kyle had many things he wanted to ask Jonah but did not want to bombard him with a mass of questions. Instead, he hoped that Jonah would freely choose to share with him.

'Yer, it's all good.' Jonah was concentrating hard on punching the bag and moving his feet, in case the bag fought back and he had to get out of the way. He still felt extremely embarrassed that Kyle saw him posing in the mirrors.

Kyle started to focus on Jonah's stance and upper body movement. 'You need to adjust your movement depending on the size of your opponent and your strategy for fighting,' he said.

Jonah stopped for a well-earned breather whilst his trainer showed him what to do.

'If they are shorter than you, especially if they have a shorter arm length, then you can stand further back,' Kyle continued. 'That allows you to hit them but keep away from their punches. However, if they are taller than you are, especially if they are much bigger, you may need to get inside their arms, up close and personal. You'll need to pile on the punches to the body at close range, looking for the uppercut punch that will knock them out.'

Jonah was curious as to why Kyle should emphasise the height and build of his opponent. Did he know about Theda? No, surely not. How could he? Jonah quickly dismissed the notion that Kyle could know anything about the evil warrior. He lowered his head and continued to hit the bag, trying the new moves Kyle had shown him.

The training session finished and Jonah felt a great sense of achievement. He had pushed himself hard and learnt new strategies and skills, for which he was grateful. He quickly showered and got dressed, ready to meet his mum.

Although Theda had been on his mind during his training, he knew that any encounter with the monster would be in a different world – the one through the Doorway. Right now, his mum was more important to him and he started to focus on his present-day life. He waited at the entrance to the community centre, a few minutes before two o'clock, looking at his watch, then through the glass doors, and then back at his watch.

'Who are you waiting for?'

The voice from behind him made Jonah jump slightly.

'Oh, 'erm, my mum. We're going out for lunch.'

'That's good,' said Kyle. 'Had any more trouble with Nat and his gang?'

'No, I haven't passed that way for a while.'

'What about your dad?'

'No, I haven't seen him either.' Jonah was paying more attention to whether his mum had arrived yet. Still, he was happy to give Kyle a few simple answers.

Kyle lowered his voice, 'And what about the evil thing you mentioned before? Is that still coming after you?'

Jonah turned and faced Kyle, now giving him his full attention. He said nothing.

'The last time we spoke you mentioned your battles with good and evil,' said Kyle. 'I was just wondering how that was going for you?'

Jonah was not sure if Kyle was making fun of him or was indeed interested in this hidden part of his life. 'Well, erm, well,' He struggled to know what to say. He wanted to share his story, especially if Kyle was genuinely interested, but his mum was due to arrive at any moment and he didn't want to start a conversation that he knew he could not finish.

'I did listen to what you said last time, about feeding the wolves and stuff, and I do want to carry on the conversation. But my mum will be here anytime now.'

Kyle understood the importance of this but he had one more question. 'Jonah, do you believe your past choices may influence your present life, or even the future?'

Jonah was not completely sure what Kyle meant. If he knew all about his travels through the Doorway, then that would be a sensible question. But how could Kyle know?

He wanted to give a quick response and replied, 'I think that what happens in one world stays in that world. It has no effect on anything else, now or in the future. Does that answer your question?'

Jonah turned to see if Beth had arrived. He felt like he had tried to answer quickly and intelligently but wasn't making sense of it at all.

'Do you think that the Master is dead?

Jonah turned quickly back to Kyle, completely surprised at the words that had just come out of his mouth. What did he mean? Kyle couldn't possibly know about the Storyteller, could he? Did he mean someone else or…?

'Hi Jonah, are you ready?' It was Beth. She had arrived, a little out of breath from rushing to be on time, and now stood at the front door of the community centre.

Jonah was still in shock at Kyle's question, unable to think of any words to respond to Kyle, or to his mum.

Silently, he moved towards the door, pushed it open, and walked out.

Beth looked at Kyle, confused. Then, not waiting for an explanation, she quickly followed her son out of the building. 'Jonah. Jonah, stop.'

He slowed down, allowing his mum to catch up with him.

'What's that all about...what's just happened?' said Beth, staring intently at Jonah. He looked stressed and anxious, his eyes staring straight ahead of him. The smiles and excitement they had shared recently were nowhere to be seen. 'Come on, tell me. What's wrong?' Beth whispered in her motherly, gentle voice, which she saved for moments like this.

Jonah could not ignore her compassionate tone. 'Everything's okay, Mum. Honest.'

'Well, it doesn't look that way to me.'

'It's just...Kyle said something that took me by surprise, that's all. Honestly, it was nothing.'

'You looked like you'd seen a ghost.'

'A ghost. There's no such thing Mum, you know that. You shouldn't believe in all that rubbish.' Jonah pretended to laugh off his mother's notion of foreign beings from spiritual worlds.

As soon as he said this, the sun disappeared behind a gathering of clouds.

***

They did not have to walk far from the community centre to the Kings Arms pub, where a succulent lunch was waiting. The short journey took them over a stile and through a small field, with the path leading them along the edge of the river to the old stone bridge opposite the pub. At the same time, both Jonah and Beth looked up and noticed large, black rainclouds quickly moving across the sky, covering the blue. Strangely, there was only a slight breeze blowing around them. This seemed to contradict the speed at which the clouds were now racing. As they watched the transformation of the skies above, they both felt the first drops of rain, simultaneously falling on their faces. A storm was not forecast on the weather reports and neither of them was prepared for getting wet.

Suddenly, a violent wind pummelled the clouds into a dark cluster and rain poured heavily on the land beneath. Thunder began to roll and several bolts of lightning threatened the trees near Beth and Jonah who were now running along the path through the fields. They reached the bridge together and began to cross the short distance to safety.

Jonah had a bad feeling about the sudden thunderstorm. He had seen the weather rapidly change like this before, but that was in the land through the Doorway. Still, now was not the time to wait around. Now was the time to get his mum safely to the sanctuary of the Kings Arms. He did not want to take any chances and believed that they would both be fine, once they reached the other side of the bridge. Unknown to him, danger was not from above this time. It was from beneath.

Theda was on the move. He had found his way through the portal to Jonah's world, and his fiery presence now caused the water in the river below the bridge to bubble. The sudden change in temperature meant that steam was rising from its surface. The giant warrior was moving quickly up through the boiling waters and nearer his target. With an outstretched arm and clenched fist, he punched his way out of the ground, through the water in the river, and straight into the old stonework construction of the bridge. As the power of his fist pushed through the aged rock, the blocks of brickwork cracked like an eggshell and started to crumble.

The force of the flying debris moving skyward knocked Beth and Jonah backwards. They were thrown off the bridge, back to where they had just been, and landed on the wet grass of the field. Theda pushed his body all the way through the stone and arrived on the edge of the river. Broken pieces of stone and brick fell, splashing into the waters below, smashing onto the path and the remaining section of bridge. Although some large fragments hit Theda, they simply bounced off him, shattering into tiny pieces. The dust settled quickly as the force of the rain pushed the crumbling bridge down, disintegrating into miniscule particles, then nothingness.

Jonah and Beth had been taken by surprise and were unprepared for their uncomfortable and painful landing.

Groaning, they both clutched various parts of their hurting bodies and tried to push themselves up off the ground.

Theda walked purposefully towards them. He did not draw his sword but kept his arms by his side.

Jonah was on his feet first; he did not have a weapon to fight and he knew, with his mum lying injured near him, they could not run away. He tried to recall a fighting strategy, from his conversations with Halecim and his previous experiences of Theda's attacks in the other world. Nothing came to mind. He had never expected Theda to follow him into his everyday life. He was without his guardian and protector, without a weapon, and now he had his mum to protect too. He adjusted his feet to gain better balance, straightened his back, tightened his recently formed muscles, and clenched his fist. A giddy concoction of fear, anger and rage induced excessive amounts of adrenaline, enabling him to move forward in an advance on his enemy. As he neared his assailant, Jonah leapt into the air and forced his fist into Theda's face. He expected his punch to hurt his own hand when it made contact with the warrior, but instead he felt nothing. Theda's face looked transparent, almost absent of any physical form.

It was like punching air!

Theda was not expecting a fight, particularly a hit from this young, smaller weakling of a human. The shock caused more concern than the punch, which only caused his head to twitch slightly. Theda turned quickly as Jonah, leaping behind him, swiftly began another assault on his opponent. This time, Theda was ready and he caught Jonah in mid-air and threw him into the sky as if he was a rugby ball.

Jonah landed on his back, a short distance from the warrior. The ground was softened by the excessive rain and his body slumped into the sodden field. He had banged his head, leaving him slightly disorientated. He tried to see through the pouring rain but could only make out the blurry figure of Theda walking towards his mum. Mustering all his strength, he stood up and could hardly believe what he was witnessing.

Theda had reached Beth, who was still on the ground where she had landed, surrounded by large clumps of stone from the bridge. He bent down and grabbed hold of her arm. She had no idea what was going on as she was barely conscious, unable to recognise the horror that was about to happen to her. In an instant, Theda, with Beth in tow, disappeared back to where he had come from, into the murky waters below.

Jonah could not do anything to stop his enemy. He felt utterly useless, powerless to protect his mum from being snatched by this evil spirit. As the rain continued to pour around him, he knelt in the muddy field, watching his mother disappear into the depths of the earth.

\*\*\*

The rain stopped falling when the storm clouds disappeared, as quickly as they arrived, leaving a clear blue sky above. The grass was soaked with the torrential rain that had fallen only moments before.

Jonah stood, his trousers covered in mud, his ankles deep in puddles of water that seeped into his trainers. His shoulders were heavy with the burden of powerlessness. His body was riddled with pain from being thrown through the air and landing hard on the ground. Worse, he could not understand what had just happened and why his mother had been taken away. In the other world, Theda had always come to attack Jonah but, this time, the dark soldier had no interest in him at all. He had only captured Jonah's mum. Why?

Across the field, from behind him, came the sound of splashing as heavy feet smashed their way through wet grass. As soon as Jonah heard the sounds, he equated them with danger. He raised his head and spun round on his left foot, his arms beginning to lift, his fingers beginning to clench. Before he needed to use a block for protection or a punch for attack, he recognised the familiar face of his friend and mentor, Kyle.

'Jonah, thank God you're okay.'

Jonah felt giddy with relief. 'Yes. I'm a bit sore but…I'm alright. Thanks.'

'What happened?' said Kyle. 'I saw storm clouds appear very quickly, just after you left the gym. Then this crazy storm appeared and disappeared in just a few minutes.'

'Yes, it was surreal.'

Kyle looked puzzled.

Jonah was not sure what he could say to explain what had just happened. He did not think it would do any good to share the true story with Kyle, but on the other hand, what else could he do? Then, he looked up and saw an expression of compassion that he had never noticed before in Kyle's face – an expression that brought back memories of how the Storyteller had looked at him when they first met. He knew the Storyteller would have a solution for this. He had to find him, as soon as possible.

'Sorry, Kyle, I've got to go.'

With that, Jonah ran as fast as his feet could carry him home. He had to reach the Doorway once again.

# 15

It did not take long for Jonah to be lifted from his bedroom floor by the strong wind pushing him through the Doorway. The last journey through the portal had been cold and unnerving. This time, its physical structure had clearly deteriorated even further. Jonah realised this must be due to the crack in time that Halecim had told him about, which seemed to be affecting the passage between the two worlds. However, he was not bothered by the icicles along the way, or the great open chasms leading to severe black holes of emptiness on either side of his path. His mind kept replaying the memory of his mum being taken from him by the evil warrior; her anxious face as she disappeared into the unknown territory of the deep while her son stood, helpless, watching her.

These harrowing thoughts were interrupted by the appearance of the huge man standing, waiting at the entrance of the Doorway for his young friend. Jonah was so pleased to see Halecim that he ran the last few steps of his journey and threw his arms around his protector, resting his head on the big guy's chest.

'He's taken my mum,' said Jonah, trying to control the choking feeling in his throat and the tears in his eyes.

'Yes, I know,' said the muscle-bound swordsman. His voice sounded warm.

Jonah released his grip and took a step backwards so that he could look at Halecim, whose gaze was full of kindness and concern. There was a slight pause as they looked at each other, as if waiting for the other to speak first.

'Jonah, I never expected this to happen,' said Halecim, at last. 'It is most unlike the enemy's usual strategy of war. I did not expect Theda to strike at Beth. It is not her time. I am waiting for the Master to tell me what to do.'

Halecim seemed agitated. It was not often that he did not know what to do or have the right answers.

'Can you take me to the Storyteller, please? I need to talk with him.' Jonah spoke quietly, calmly, and very politely.

'Of course.'

Halecim was not going to make Jonah walk across the hot, dusty desert and mountain ranges again, so he reached out his hand and placed it on Jonah's wrist. 'Hold tight,' he said, before moving off at an astronomical speed.

*** 

Jonah had gone through this experience so many times before that his mind was now focused less on the speed at which he was travelling and more on his destination. Soon, he hoped to be face to face with the Storyteller.

They came to rest on a luscious green hillside, overlooking the huge lake that now seemed calm and peaceful. It looked very different to when Jonah had witnessed the crashing waves of the storm, the last time he was here. This time, with his feet firmly fixed on the ground, Jonah appreciated the view; the spectacular scenery of an exquisite part of the world he never grew tired of seeing.

Halecim raised his arm and pointed a little way further up the hillside. 'He's just over there,' he said to Jonah. 'I'll wait here for you. Take your time.'

Jonah left Halecim behind him as he made his way up the hill. Passing small and large clusters of rocks, carefully stepping over sharp, rugged boulders to avoid twisting his ankle, Jonah made his way towards a large, craggy area. He stood near the base of a rock face that looked huge but was realistically only about fifteen feet high. He contemplated climbing it but decided to look for an alternative way up, rather than risk falling off at this point. On closer inspection, he noticed a hidden crack on the left-hand side of the rock and, peering through, he saw it opened out into a wider route that led up to the top of the crag. Whilst squeezing through the crack, then pulling himself up on the dusty, dirty rocks, he wondered why it was such a mission to reach the Storyteller. Why couldn't Halecim take him straight there, or why couldn't they meet on the beach below? It seemed a little unnecessary, considering the rest of the journey Jonah had been through. However, he continued to the top, ignoring the dust clinging to his trousers and trainers.

***

Reaching the top of this little rocky area on the hillside gave Jonah a slight sense of achievement. He stood upright and began to try to brush the dust and dirt off his clothes. A sudden, strange sense of someone else being present made him stop what he was doing. He slowly raised his head. There before him was the Storyteller: the one whom he had been longing to talk to for such a long time; the one whom Halecim, the great warrior, called Master. Many times, Jonah had thought about the words he would use when this moment finally arrived, especially after Theda had snatched his mum away from him. Now, the moment had come, Jonah did not know what to do. Should he bow, or offer his hand to be shaken? He felt slightly unworthy of being in this man's presence, as though he had an audience with the Queen, and felt awkward dressed in his dirty jeans and trainers.

'Hello Jonah, I've been expecting you,' said the Storyteller.

'That's strange. Those were the words Halecim used the first time I met him, although he said we, not I,' Jonah thought.

'We've met briefly before, on the boat, and I'm sorry we didn't have a chance to talk in more depth then.'

Jonah looked slightly embarrassed, 'I know, er…Sir?' He was not sure how to address the Storyteller but continued anyway. 'And I'm sorry that you were woken from your sleep. But thank you for scaring off Theda. I don't know how you did it but…thank you.'

'A lot has happened to you in the past few weeks and I am sure you must have many questions for me, but now is not the right time to discuss them. Especially as you have more pressing issues,' said the Storyteller.

'Yes, you're right. I do have some questions. But, first, I need to know where my mum is, and how to get her back.' Jonah could feel his worry and confusion creeping into his voice.

The Storyteller sat down on the ground and gestured for Jonah to sit next to him. 'Jonah, you need to know that your mum has done nothing wrong. She is being used as bait, a way to get to you.'

'But why?'

'Since time was created, Vilde has believed that he can win the war against the Creator. Even though he was made a beautiful creature in the first place, and was given the highest job of looking after this world and all that is in it, that was not enough for him. He wanted to be worshipped rather than bow down before the Lord and Creator.'

'So, why didn't the Creator kill him?'

'Because the Creator is not only a judge and a ruler, he is a compassionate Father too. He is loving and caring. He was pleased with what he had created and, although Vilde didn't do what he wanted, he did not want to destroy him. If that had been the case, he would have built robots with no soul, no ability to choose, and with no heart to love. No, the Creator wants everyone he creates to love him because they choose to, because of his love for them as a Father. He creates a Father-shaped hole in their lives, a hole that only he can fill.'

'My dad isn't caring and loving,' Jonah's reply had a bitter tone to it.

'Your dad made unwise choices based on human emotions. It takes a very strong man to resist the things that tempt him, even if he knows that he will hurt other people. Even those who ask for His help can still make the wrong choices. Your dad ...'

Jonah interrupted the Storyteller. 'I don't want to talk about my dad. It's my mum I'm here for.'

'Of course, Jonah. We will carry on that conversation later.'

The Storyteller paused for a moment, as if pondering how much he should say, then continued: 'Vilde uses a wide variety of tools and weapons to keep humans separated and alienated from the Creator. He is very sly and cunning, working behind the scenes through human emotion, thought and behaviour. He tries to persuade people that the Creator doesn't exist or, if he does exist, that he doesn't love them, that he is a cruel tyrant. Vilde gains his strength from the doubt and disbelief that he causes, and he continues until he has completely turned a person's heart cold. He crushes hope and squeezes out love. He uses fear, pain, and guilt as his weapons for mass destruction of the human race. You, Jonah, have been on

Vilde's priority list since you first discovered the Doorway in your bedroom. He watched you move in and out of the hidden world, knowing that it would not be long before you came back in time to find me. Vilde is powerful but he has many weaknesses and flaws. He can only see what is present and can only be in one place at a time. That is why he has been building an army of demons and fallen angels over many centuries.'

'How do you know all of this, and why should I believe you?' asked Jonah, with the greatest of respect for this man whose presence oozed authority and grandeur – even if his plain clothes did not!

'I am the Creator's Son. I was there at the beginning. That is why I know Vilde so well.'

Jonah had no idea how to respond to this last statement. He found it hard to grasp the concept of this man sitting next to him now actually being around since the beginning of time. He had every reason to doubt the Storyteller but he also knew he needed to start believing in something, or someone, or else he would lose his chance to get his mum back. So, if this was some kind of war between good and evil, he felt that the Storyteller (who seemed so kind and patient) must indeed be on the side of good. That was important if he was going to enter a battle against the evil Vilde.

'How can this beast live so long?' asked Jonah, puzzling about Vilde being present from the beginning of time.

'Oh, he was not always evil. He was created as an angel, an arch-angel to be precise, to watch over the earth. There was only one other arch-angel created to watch over the spiritual heaven, where good and evil angels battle, and you already know him. He goes by the name of Halecim.'

Jonah's look of shock and surprise brought a smile to the Storyteller's face. Then he continued, 'I know this may be hard to hear, and even more difficult to understand, but Theda was able to travel through the time-rift because you constantly chose to believe that I was nothing more than an ordinary man. You did not see that I have the power to —'

'Halecim's an angel? With wings?' Jonah interrupted, not really listening to anything else.

'Yes Jonah, but you need to pay attention to what I'm saying,' said the Storyteller.

'No wonder we moved so quickly. I thought he just ran really, really fast.'

'Jonah!'

The Storyteller's commanding tone made Jonah jump. It was not a shout or even said with a raised voice. It was simply his name spoken with authority. Jonah snapped out of his thoughts and looked at the man who had commanded his full attention with the simplest of words.

'Sorry sir, I mean… sorry,' he spluttered.

'That's okay, Jonah. I know this is not easy, but you must pay full attention if you want to get you mother back. You found the Doorway at your greatest point of need, when your dad rejected you, remember? It was not long after the time you stood on the railway bridge. Having the Doorway was a special gift. It gave you the opportunity to regularly escape from your painful feelings and, after a while, you found me. However, over the last few months, Vilde has been watching with interest to see if you would make his job of destroying you easier, or more difficult. He did not want to take any chances and that is why he sent Theda to kill you, the first time you came through the Doorway into this world. Fortunately, the Creator can see everything and he knew Vilde's plan, so he sent Halecim to fight off Theda and scare him away. That would have succeeded but things changed in the time-rift when you saw me at work but did not believe it was anything other than a trick or an illusion. That unbelief damaged the portal and the more you disbelieved, the weaker the portal became. Eventually, on the boat, when you still thought that you could fight Theda on your own, even when I was there right next to you, it gave Vilde the power to shatter the gateway between the worlds.'

Jonah sat and listened to all this, his emotions changing from embarrassment to alarm, then to confusion and more embarrassment. Trying to defend himself he blurted out, 'But I was the only one who stood up to Theda on the boat. All the other blokes were too weak and scared.'

'Yes, they were scared,' said the Storyteller, 'but with good reason. They knew their humanity was weak when pitched against such evil powers. You, on the other hand, believed in your own ability to battle the dark warrior…to fight him alone, with your newly formed strength that you gained from only a couple of sessions at the local gym.'

When the Storyteller mentioned the gym, he smiled as if he knew all about Jonah's attempts to boost his muscles. Then he said, 'The difference between you and the fishermen in the boat is, very simply…they knew they needed me, and you didn't.'

'So? What's the problem with that? I don't need anyone. I can look after myself.' Jonah did not like admitting that he needed anyone's help, even though he knew deep down it was true.

'The Creator brought you into this world as an expression of his love and desire for relationship, like a father with his children,' said the Storyteller. 'You cannot exist on your own. You were not made that way. The other men in the boat knew they needed help from someone who could challenge Theda and that is why they came to me. Their failing was thinking that, while in my immediate presence, they were still in danger. Their human emotions stopped them believing the Creator has given me the authority to save them.'

'What do you mean?' asked Jonah, less defiant now.

'Theda would not have attacked once he knew I was on the boat. He may think he has some power over me – though he will soon discover the limits of his power – but as he drew closer to the boat, he saw me and left. He knows that his time to fight has not come.'

Jonah was confused. He was not sure what questions he should be asking anymore. The Storyteller seemed very patient with him, not getting exasperated or frustrated as Halecim usually did, but watching and waiting for him to grasp what was being said.

'I know this is hard to understand. Believe me, everyone finds this difficult, but only because you make it far more complicated than it really is. You fight against belief in my ability to heal peoples' broken bodies and souls, and your need to let me become involved in your life. You think that, if you do this, you will lose control of your life and choices.

This startled Jonah. Could the Storyteller read his mind?

'You are not the only one to think this,' continued the Storyteller. 'Since the creation of the world, humanity has struggled with this, and resisted seeing the Creator as a Father who loves his children and wants them to get the best out of life.'

After saying this, the Storyteller looked sad. He became very still and they both sat there in silence for a while.

For Jonah, things were becoming a little clearer. 'I didn't realise the Doorway was there to help me through my nightmares,' he said. 'I'm sorry that I didn't really believe in you being more than an ordinary man, or that you had divine powers. I thought you were just clever with juggling tricks! And I had no idea that my attitude had anything to do with letting Theda climb through the time-rift and take my mum. I know I can't get her back on my own, and I'm really grateful that you sent Halecim to help me. I just wish I could understand everything better so I can make the right choices and not feel I'm doing this on my own.'

'Jonah, you are not alone. You have many angels, as well as Halecim, fighting alongside you and helping you to understand. There will come a time when you will be able to know the Creator properly, not as an authority figure telling you what to do, but as a father who truly loves you. Until then, go and get your mum back.'

The Storyteller stood to his feet and Jonah stood too, quietly waiting for a few moments as he looked up into the Storyteller's kind face. The sense of connection between them was so intense, it was almost overpowering and Jonah could feel his eyes brimming up with tears. Then the Storyteller gently raised his arm and pointed, encouraging him to turn around.

Without Jonah knowing, Halecim had arrived and was standing behind him.

Jonah hastily hid his tears as he bent to wipe the dust from his clothes then, raising his head with a cheeky smile, started to tease his friend.

'So, you have wings, eh?'

'Yes,' came the reply and, as the word left his lips, Halecim slowly revealed his impressive set of feathers. They were huge, each spanning an impressive twelve feet from top to bottom; purest white with soft, velvety plumes. They gently swayed in the mountain breeze and looked amazing in the warm light of sunset.

The moment was truly a special one, even if it came in the shadow of dark times to come.

When Jonah turned back to say something else to the Storyteller, he was surprised to see that he had disappeared.

'Don't worry,' said Halecim. 'You'll see him again very soon. Now it's time for us to go too.' Then the winged warrior held out his hand for Jonah to grab.

\*\*\*

As they travelled, the sun set and the moon began to glimmer, reflecting the sparkling light from the millions of stars that had appeared in the sky. The wind picked up and was blowing hard, but Halecim's strong open wings protected Jonah from its effects as they gracefully swayed backwards and forwards, then upwards and downwards, before the wind lifted them off the ground and took them swiftly from the mountain to the lower lands that overlooked the sea.

Halecim pointed towards the middle of a large lake where a storm was stirring the waters. 'Can you see the sailors in the boats out there? They are having a rough time rowing against the strong wind. They can't use their sails as that will take them in the opposite direction to where the Storyteller has told them to meet him. Let's join them to see what happens'

'I'm glad we don't have to walk now,' said Jonah, laughing with relief, 'but won't the men in the boat see us?'

'Don't worry. Your new belief has repaired some of the portal damage and we will, once again, be invisible to them,' said Halecim.

This appeared to be true for, as soon as their feet touched down at the back of the boat, nobody took any notice of them. Instead, the sailors were frantically rowing with all their strength. Suddenly, one of them stopped and hysterically began shaking his outstretched arm at something he could see in the water. The other men followed their friend's gaze. What they saw made them all stop rowing and stand up in the boat. They could hardly believe their eyes.

Jonah knew it was the Storyteller walking towards the boat but he could see that the sailors were terrified.

'It's a ghost,' shouted one of them.

It could be the only explanation for it. They were in the middle of a huge lake and they saw the outline of a man walking on the water towards them. Although he was not very far from the boat, they struggled to recognise it was the Storyteller. Their fear forced them to conclude that it must be a ghost coming to frighten them.

Seeing their terrified, shaking bodies covered in sweat, the ghost-figure said, 'Take courage. It is I. Do not be afraid.'

Immediately, the men recognised the voice of their master and leader. A great sigh of relief went around the boat as, one by one, they each realised they were safe, and not about to be torn apart by an evil spirit.

One of the men in the boat shouted back, 'My Lord, if it is you, let me come to you.'

Jonah watched amazed as the Storyteller summoned the man, who climbed over the side of the boat and began to put his feet in the water.

Another sailor grabbed his arm. 'What are you doing? Don't be a fool,' he said.

The man in the water turned his head and fixed his eyes on the ghost-like figure before him. As the fisherman took each step, he slowly began to grow in confidence, unable to comprehend that he was walking on water. However, his confidence in his own ability to overcome the natural elements soon disappeared when the wind suddenly smashed into him, and he quickly began to sink into the water. Consumed with fear again, he cried out for help. With an outstretched arm, the Storyteller came to his rescue, pulled him up out of the sea, and took him to the side of the boat. There, they were both helped on board by the other boatmen. As soon as their feet touched the deck, the wind died down and the waters became calm again.

Although the men were relieved that it was not a ghost, the realisation that they had just seen their leader walking on water completely amazed them. They were all speechless. A couple of them consoled the one who had ended up with very wet feet and was now feeling exceptionally embarrassed. The rest of the sailors stood still, not knowing what to say to the Storyteller.

Jonah and Halecim had been watching the drama unfold from where they sat, invisible, at the back of the boat. Jonah did not need an explanation as to how the Storyteller could walk on water. He now realised that, as the Creator's Son, he had power to control nature. That was why he could stop the storm the last time Jonah was on a boat with him.

'Halecim, why are these men so surprised that he can walk on water? Surely, if they've followed him for a while, they've seen him perform other supernatural miracles. I know. I've seen them.'

Although they were invisible to the others in the boat, Halecim kept his voice low, just in case the portal rift had not repaired the sound deflectors. 'These men may have spent the past two years with the Storyteller, and heard many amazing stories and seen many miracles, but they still do not fully understand his presence on earth. The one who joined him on the water has a stronger faith that helped him climb out of the boat in the first place, but when he was at his weakest on the water, he still relied on his own strength rather than look to the Master. You need to remember that.'

It sounded like a warning.

As Jonah pondered this, he heard Halecim whisper, 'Are you ready? It's time to leave.'

Jonah did not feel ready but, as he gently grabbed hold of Halecim's arm for take-off, he took a final glance towards the Storyteller who offered a calming and supportive wink of his eye, and a smile.

It was time to fly into battle and rescue Beth.

# 16

Pulling the zip back and reaching into his bag, Kyle fumbled with the contents until he found his soft, fluffy, white towel. Still soaking wet from the storm, he had returned to the gym to dry off. Rubbing the towel vigorously over his head, he did not hear the door open, or the young man who walked in and stood close behind him.

As Kyle wiped his face, the reflection of the teenager in the walled mirrors suddenly caught his eye. He slowly turned his head towards the boy. With most of his face still covered by the towel, he spoke quietly. 'Hello Nathan. I didn't expect to see you in here.'

Kyle was the only person who used Nat's full name. Not even Nat's mother used it when she was angry with him; she was too afraid of his reaction. He had never liked the name she gave him. Kyle and Nat had developed a relationship in the boxing club over the past twelve years but it had turned sour. Ever since Nat had used his fighting skills to abuse, bully and scare other people with his gang in town, he had fallen out of favour with Kyle. He had also lost all respect from the regulars in the gym.

'I need to talk,' said Nat. 'Have you got a minute?'

Kyle noticed that Nat looked embarrassed and uncomfortable in his presence. This was a huge step for Nat. He must have been desperate to put himself through the shame of walking into the gym where he was not welcome. 'Take a seat,' he said and pointed to a white plastic chair. Then, he sat down and waited for Nat to take the chair opposite him.

They looked across the table at each other, waiting for the other to speak first. Finally, the silence was broken by Nat who nervously stuttered a few words.

'I'm…erm…ssss…ser-cared. I mean…I, I'm scared, Kyle.'

'Scared? Of what?'

'Of what I've become,' said Nat.

'What have you become?' asked Kyle.

'A mer…monster.'

Nathan held his head in his hands in shame. He was usually quite descriptive in his use of vocabulary but, today, his apparent disgust at himself, and what he had become, was robbing him of words.

'What makes you a monster, Nathan?'

Raising his head from his hands, Nat looked at Kyle's caring face and realised he was not being judged. This was the only person he felt he could trust to share his deep pain. For the first time in his life, he wanted to be open and honest.

'I know I've done many bad things in my life…hurting people just for fun or entertainment…making others live in fear of me and causing pain…not just physically, but emotionally too. And I've led others to do the same terrible things.'

'And why does this make you a monster?' asked Kyle.

'Because I'm scary. Because people are afraid of me. Because I'm evil.' Nat hung his head in shame again.

'You're not evil,' said Kyle.

'Yes, I am. I know I am.'

'No. You may do evil things…but that doesn't make you evil. Though it does mean you need to change the choices you've been making,' said Kyle, carefully.

'I know what I am. You don't have to put a positive spin on it,' said Nat, who was secretly convinced that he was evil, through and through.

'Then, why are you here Nat?'

'Erm…it was…a couple of weeks ago. This lad walked onto our patch and we thought we'd have some fun with him, pushing him around, laughing at him, all that. But then, without any warning he suddenly clenched his fist and punched three of the lads, knocking them to the floor. Well, the rest of the boys went ballistic. They started to lay into him. It got very messy.'

'And what did you do?' asked Kyle.

'To be honest, I was in shock. I stood there for a few seconds, amazed at this boy's courage, or stupidity, to fight us all. Eventually, I snapped out of my spaced state and called the boys off.'

'Why?'

'No-one has ever stood up to me before, let alone taken on all of us. There was something different about this lad, something special that I've only ever seen once before. He may not have had the physical strength to beat us all, but that didn't stop him. His heart and soul were strong, and he was prepared to stand up…to fight for what was right.'

So, where have you seen that before?'

'In you, Kyle. Why do you think I'm back here?'

Kyle was silent.

'You're the only one who has ever challenged me to think about inner strength and try to understand right from wrong.'

Still, Kyle was silent. He waited, knowing that there were more words to come.

'I don't want to be evil. I don't want to hurt people anymore, but…but, I don't know what to do.'

Kyle felt compassion for the broken boy sitting hunched in front of him. He could tell Nat was full of remorse about his actions and choices; he seemed to be genuine in wanting to stop and change his life. Kyle smiled gently before speaking, doing his best to make eye contact.

'Nat, you need to think carefully about what you are saying. If you want to change your behaviour and leave the path of destruction you've been pursuing, you will upset many people who look up to you and think what you do is cool. And there will be others who rely on you to do their dirty work for them. What about their criminal exploits? Are you prepared to become unpopular, to deal with anger and other negative feelings…because these people won't understand or like the new choices you make?'

'Yes Kyle, I am. I can't carry on my life with all this hatred and pain inside me. I need to find out if there is something more than this, a purpose for my life, a reason for my existence. I need to find out what that is, rather than waste away…hurting people instead. There has to be a better way.'

***

It was a late summer evening as Nat walked along the main road, with the boxing ring behind him and the estate in front of him. After a long conversation with Kyle, who had listened patiently for hours and never interrupted, Nat left the gym feeling peaceful and pleased with the direction that he had now chosen to take. He knew he had some difficult choices to make but he had found strength and courage in talking to Kyle and knew that he was not alone. He had never felt like this before. Now he had a deep sense of relief as he believed, for the first time in his life, that he was not evil. There was a purpose to his life. It was the happiest he had been for as long as he could remember.

This special moment did not last long.

As Nat turned a corner, walking into one of the many alleyways on the estate, he was horrified to see his friends attacking a lonely, isolated boy who had obviously taken the wrong turning, venturing onto the gang's turf. He had seen it many times before when someone was so absorbed in their mobile phone, watching the screen and listening to the music blasting through their earphones, they did not realise where they were going. By the time they had taken the wrong turning, it was too late for them to turn back. This must have been the fate of the frightened youth now cowering on the floor. The group of boys surrounding their victim were demanding his phone and wallet.

Nat knew the usual response of scared teenagers on their own was to simply hand over their precious possessions and run off, as quickly as possible. Lately, this had changed. Over the past couple of weeks, the rumours of Jonah fighting Nat's fearful gang had spread and some brave lads had decided that they could follow Jonah's example and stand up to the gang too. This was one of those times. This particular boy didn't want to hand over his phone and refused the aggressive demands to give it away.

The gang did not take rejection well and they were becoming increasingly concerned about losing their credibility and reputation for spreading fear. They needed to send a message to the community. So, they started to beat the boy with their fists and kick him violently. Six against one wasn't great odds and their weak, vulnerable victim lay on the floor with his knees bent up to his chest and his arms and hands covering his head.

'Arggh', 'Ow', 'thud', and other painful noises started to fill the air, this time not from the helpless boy cringing on the pavement but from the bullies and thugs as they landed with great force against the walls of the alleyway, cracking their heads on the brickwork before sliding down to the ground.

'Nat, what are you doing?' shouted one of them.

The gang could hardly believe their eyes as their own leader was grabbing his friends one at a time, holding on to their trousers with one hand and the clothes around their necks with the other, and flinging them far away from their prey. Four of them had been thrown to the floor before anyone had realised what was going on. The two remaining lads, Dan and Kane, stopped their beating of the boy having realised that their partners in crime were lying around them in pain. They saw Nat coming towards them and it was Dan who had cried out in astonishment 'Nat, what are you doing?'

Nat was in no mood for talking. He was horrified when he had witnessed what his gang was doing to the boy on the ground. Something had changed in him since the violent attack on Colin a few days before. When he witnessed their violent actions again this evening, it made him feel sick in his stomach and intensely angry.

The gang had become worried about Nat since they had stopped his fun the last time. Now his violent behaviour towards them was confusing. Why had he become so unpredictable? Though Dan and Kane were still standing, they flinched as Nat came towards them and they both moved away quickly from the boy bleeding on the floor. Crouching down, Nat helped the wounded boy to his feet.

By now the others had stood up, rubbing the areas of their body that still hurt.

'What are you doing Nat. You're supposed to be on our side?'

'Why aren't you joining in Nat?'

'You've changed.'

One after the other, the gang members fired these questions at Nat, not understanding why he was behaving so weirdly this evening.

'You're our leader Nat, what's going on?' said Dan, remembering the last time he challenged Nat and how he nearly had a knife through his face. This time he kept his distance, just in case.

Nat had ignored everyone while he focused his attention on getting the wounded boy to his feet but hearing Dan's words made him raise his head towards his friend and look him straight in the eyes. 'This has got to stop.'

It was a simple reply but one that neither Dan or any of the others understood. Then Nat put his arm around the injured lad's waist, helping him to walk away.

Dan continued to shout questions as his friend left them behind. 'What do you mean? This isn't going to stop. This is our war Nat, our fight against everything that's wrong with this place. It's not over, not by a long shot. If you're not with us Nat, then you're against us. Remember that. It's your choice, Nat.'

Even though Dan continued to shout, Nat refused to turn around and acknowledge him. He chose to walk away from his brother-in-arms, walk away as a stranger, an enemy even. It made him sad, but he knew it was something he had to do.

# 17

Jonah and Halecim reached the Doorway, a familiar sight for them both. For the warrior, it was the exit from one world to the next. For the young traveller, it was usually the way home, but not now. There was a strangeness about this journey. Both were uncertain about where they would end up, what would happen next, and if they would return safely with Beth.

Halecim pushed the door open and ushered Jonah through. As the young man stood between his protector and the old wooden door, he stopped and looked into Halecim's eyes. 'Are we going to make it?'

Halecim gave a reassuring smile. 'Your journey has been teaching you about faith. Now is the time to believe that we will return.'

This was enough to comfort Jonah and boost his confidence to go through the Doorway into the unknown. Halecim followed swiftly, and as the light behind them disappeared, Halecim guided them forward along the shadowy corridor of time. They walked next to each other, although Jonah had to keep taking twice as many steps to keep up with Halecim's huge strides. He reached out to grab his protector's arm, not through fear of the dark but because he did not want to lose contact with his friend. He was starting to put his faith into practice. He had to believe that his guardian angel would get them through this new challenge on their tough journey.

Moving forward, Jonah felt a strong wind pressing against them. He realised the Doorway had been drastically changing during his last couple of trips, and this was even worse. Before, the wind had always been behind him, gently pushing him towards his exit point. This time, the wind seemed to be trying to prevent them both from reaching their destination. Jonah had to keep his eyes tightly shut, to protect them from the sting of the howling wind. He did not need to see, as it was pitch black everywhere. When later, he tried to peer into the gloom, he noticed a glimmer of pale, brownish light approaching in the distance, swirling in circles as though a torch was being swung around someone's head. Very quickly, this strange new light reached them and, upon its arrival, propelled the two travellers out of the Doorway's exit into a sandstorm. The ferocious wind sent them both flying as they tumbled into each other and landed on the deep, hot sand.

Jonah tried to see what was happening but the sand clung to his half-open eyelids. Very quickly, he raised his left arm to cover his face. Halecim stood up, shaken that the Doorway had so forcefully expelled them from its territory. He walked the twenty or so feet towards Jonah, then opened his wings to cover them both. The sound of the raging wind became muted and Jonah stopped feeling the sting from the clouds of sand smashing into his skin. He was not sure what had happened but, lowering his arm, he was just about able to see the friendly face of his companion.

'Are you okay?' came the caring voice of his protector.

'Yes, I'm okay. Where are we?'

'A place no-one should ever be. In Hell.'

Jonah did not expect to hear such stern, solemn words. He knew they were going to rescue his mum from a dark place, but he had never thought it would be Hell, or that Hell was a real place anyway.

'This is not somewhere we should stay longer than we have to. We must be on our guard at all times,' said Halecim.

A thought struck Jonah. 'Have you been here before?' he asked.

'No,' said Halecim. 'Many angels made the choice to follow Vilde when he first rebelled against the Creator and so they were all thrown into this horrific place. But I have never been here before.'

'And where, exactly, is Hell?'

'In another dimension, a place separated from the universe in which you currently live. It is a place where only the unbelieving dead and Vilde's followers can exist – the only place in the whole of creation where the Creator does not choose to come. Now that we are here, we need to be very, very careful.'

Jonah had not truly understood before how dangerous this present journey would be. He had presumed it would be safe because he had his guardian angel with him. But now, for the first time, he noticed a difference in Halecim, something strange in his eyes; not fear exactly, but there was an uncertainty that was not usually there. He was worried. Did the Storyteller make the right decision to send them into Vilde's dark world?

'Come on. We need to start moving. Stay close.' Halecim's words were quiet but stern. If he feared the horrors and battles that might lie ahead of them, it was still clear he had been given a task and he would continue in obedience to do his best to guard Jonah with his life.

It was time for them to move forward, in unison, to rescue Beth.

***

They walked in the hot, burning sand for hours. Jonah's feet hurt so much he had let the winged warrior lift him onto his shoulders and now he clung to his neck. He dipped his head into the giant, feathered wings to shelter, not just from the force of the swirling sandstorm which never ceased, but also the searing heat from the ball of fire above them. It could be described as the sun but it's not as far away as the sun is from the earth Jonah thought, when he peeped his head out to have a look. No, this was a ball of fire that hovered close to the land they walked on, producing a scorching heat. Halecim had warned Jonah that it was intended to burn the flesh off the bones of all who ventured into its territory – to inflict maximum pain.

Despite this, Halecim did not seem to suffer any pain, even though the tips of his feathers were turning brown with the fire burning around them.

Safe within the comfort of the winged shield, Jonah asked, 'Why don't we fly?'

Halecim stopped for a moment to lower his head beneath the folded wings and answer the question. 'This is a very dangerous place. As I've never been here before, I'm not sure what to expect. There could be armed demons patrolling the skies or vehicles hovering over the desolate sands. If we fly, I am sure we will bring more attention to ourselves, so we will walk.'

After this, Jonah decided not to continue with the questions and wait until they found somewhere to escape the sandstorm. At the summit of the next dune, Halecim crouched down. This was a bit difficult and clumsy, with Jonah clinging to his shoulders and his head still tucked under his wings. It gave Jonah a jolt.

'What?' shouted Jonah.

'Sssh!' came the reply.

Jonah peered out over the top of the wings to see before him what looked like a ghost town. It reminded him of the towns he'd seen in old cowboy movies but this one was completely derelict, with two rows of wooden buildings facing each other across a narrow street. The buildings were an odd assortment of shapes and sizes and Jonah tried to count them. He thought there might be twelve on the left and thirteen on the right, but it was difficult to see properly through the swirling sand and the glaze caused by the heat of the flames that surrounded the town and the path before them.

'We have to go into that town. There is a hidden entrance there, which leads to the depths of the underworld, and we need to find it,' said Halecim, trying to whisper but needing to raise his voice above the sound of the wind.

There was no more explanation about what to expect on their journey but Jonah knew that it did not matter what difficulties or challenges lay before them. They could not turn back now. He resumed his tight grip around Halecim's neck, standing up again on the angel's huge feet, as they began their journey into the ghost town.

***

Shivering with cold, and fearful of the strange blue and red flames that blazed in every direction she looked, Beth found herself unable to move. She was tied to a pole: eight-foot tall and scorched black from the flames that burned but gave no heat. Her hands were forced behind her back, tied extremely tightly with thick rope rubbing her wrists. The pain was excruciating. Still, this was nothing compared to the burning pain in her knees. After two days of being on her feet, she was unable to remain standing any longer. She slid down the pole, her knees forced into the hot ash, her body slumped forward, with her arms bent behind her back and still tied to the pole.

Her eyes were swollen from her constant crying since she had been taken from the earth. Now beyond tears, exhausted, she quivered when she heard the screeching, horrific sound that she had come to dread: the sound of Theda coming towards her.

Since arriving in this pit of despair, she had been constantly tortured by seven demons that guarded the circular platform on which she now knelt. Each of the demons had shrivelled skin, horribly stained and disfigured by the pit of fire in which they had lived for thousands of years. They crouched and slithered all over the ash-covered floor, each taking it in turns to quickly move towards Beth and assault their captive with slaps, punches and kicks. However, when Theda appeared from the shadowy depths, moving silently towards the middle of the cave, the creatures moved away in fear, bowing with their heads low to the ground, dragging their distorted noses through the ash.

Theda's black coat caused a swirl of dust as he speedily moved towards his victim. He stood only a few inches away from Beth. She looked down at his black feet and the hem of his grimy cloak. His loud, deep breathing was almost masked by the sound of snivelling, scared demons and the raging fire. Beth slowly lifted her head, looking at Theda's face in one last act of defiance. She had no voice left to scream with, no more tears to cry, and she was numb with pain. After a few seconds, she dropped her head again. There was nothing to be said. Battered and bruised, Beth was a broken woman.

It would only be a matter of time before Theda had won the victory. He walked away, smirking. Job done.

***

The sandstorm came to a sudden and abrupt stop as Jonah and Halecim stepped into the abandoned town. It was as if a wall of glass had separated the elements of wind and fire, as they left the storms of the desert and faced the plumes of flames on the streets before them. Halecim lowered Jonah to the ground. As Jonah stepped onto the hot surface of the pavement below, he could feel the heat starting to melt the rubber soles of his trainers.

Halecim reached behind his back, parted his wings and, from between his spine and feathers, pulled two full-length, jet black cloaks, and some protective covers for Jonah's shoes. He handed the shoes and one of the cloaks to Jonah. 'Put these on,' he said.

Jonah stretched the covers over his trainers and flung his cloak over his shoulders at the same time as Halecim pulled the other cloak over his massive feathered wings and muscular arms. They both put their hoods up simultaneously and, with a renewed confidence, they felt ready to move forward.

Before they took their next step, they felt a strange sensation on their arms as something brushed past them. It was cold, felt creepy, and sent shivers down Jonah's back, sending his body into a spasm. He felt sick with the stench that followed behind a grotesque cluster of indescribable creatures that flew swiftly by.

It was hard to identify the size, shape or number of limbs on each of the abominations. The skin on these creatures was charred from the constant flames burning around them, but still hair grew uncontrollably in all areas of their body. Two of them had bony torsos, with wasted lumps of skin protruding from their backs, like tails. Three had huge mouths, flashing jagged teeth that were either dirty yellow, or black. *They definitely don't have a dentist in this place*, thought Jonah, as he tried to distract himself from the terrible noises that came from the creatures when they passed in front of him and faded into the distance. Their voices sounded scared and tormented, as if they feared some dreadful punishment.

'That was horrible,' said Jonah when the creatures had gone. 'What were they?'

'Those, Jonah, are demons and, yes, they are horrible,' said Halecim. 'They are Godless evil beings with nothing good, or honest, left in them at all. They move between this world and yours, causing havoc and convincing humans to do wrong.'

'Why couldn't they see us?' Jonah asked.

'These cloaks have a protective cover so that the demons are unable to see us. The outside of each cloak has been stained with the dark vices which the demons find normal in their world, so they won't suspect anything unusual, clean or pure is in their presence. There are many more demons ahead of us, some extremely dangerous. Although they cannot see us, we need to be careful as we move through the town.'

They continued the journey with Halecim taking the lead and Jonah always half a step behind him, almost jogging to keep up. The hems and edges of their cloaks glowed orange as the surrounding fire tried to set them alight. As they came closer to the town, they saw a mass of demons, evil spirits and ghost-like shapes darting frantically between the buildings. Jonah could hear them all making a lot of noise but struggled to make out what they were talking about.

Halecim reached the first wooden building which was enveloped with flames. This was a strange phenomenon for, although the flames were of fire, the wood was not scorched or turning to charcoal. The flames seemed to perpetually hover over the building without burning it.

Jonah knew there were many things about this place that he would not understand so he decided to choose carefully which questions he should ask Halecim next. Wood that did not burn was a magic trick he did not need an answer for right now!

'Stay close, very close,' commanded Halecim, ushering Jonah to his side.

They waited for a gap in the movement of spirits and then made a dash to get through the thick traffic, running in front of the first building and stopping before the next. The demons and spirits were moving between buildings in neat, horizontal lines – as though they were following invisible roads in mid-air. They appeared to be travelling in regimental order as if responding to a higher command. The noise was horrendously loud, a mixture of crackling wood, sizzling fire and the manic, crazed voices of demons shouting at each other.

As things hotted up, Halecim tilted his head and started mouthing words that Jonah could not hear properly. Then he suddenly darted ahead, through a small gap between the buildings. Instinctively, Jonah followed but he was too slow to catch up and instead had to push against the sinister creatures that were banging into him, shoving him backwards and forwards.

The wispy spirits seemed to bounce off his cloak but the demons, who felt heavier than the spirits, kept hitting Jonah as they knocked him out of their way. Although there were hundreds of them, moving at great speed, they only seemed to hit him one at a time. This changed when a large gathering of these evil anomalies linked together as one giant beast and flew straight in his direction. As the beast passed Jonah, its force swept over him and whisked him along into a burning building, up the steps, and through the saloon-style doors.

Jonah felt pain, deep pain, but it was not in his body, or caused by the physical strength of the beast. Instead he felt an inner pain, a deep ache hurting inside that he had never felt before, so painful that it brought tears to his eyes. He was not sure what he had expected to see in the building, maybe a bar, or people sitting around playing cards and drinking whisky, like they did in the cowboy films. Through his watery eyes, he managed to look around the room and there was nothing, and no-one there. All he could see was a black whirlwind, swirling around in the empty space. He felt a physical pain in his right arm followed by a tight squeeze and, with headlong speed, he was pulled back towards the doors and out of the building. Halecim had rescued his friend again.

Jonah found himself on the ground in an alley at the back of the buildings, where it was much quieter, away from the chaos in the town.

'Are you okay, Jonah?' the friendly giant asked in a soft tone, leaning over him.

'What happened?' said Jonah, through gasps.

'There are hundreds of thousands of different forms of evil in this place. You have just encountered Legion.'

'Sorry. What?' said Jonah, confused already.

'Legion. It's the name given to a large cluster of evil, interconnected spirits that form into a powerful mass and merge and twist together. As Legion passed you, it had the power to lift you into that building in its trail.'

'What is that building? It's definitely not a cowboy saloon!'

'No. It's a portal back into your world,' Halecim explained. 'This is how the demons cross from one territory to the next. They are given instructions about which humans to target, and how to provoke and entice them to act in ways that go against my Master's way of life. They are all very good at their job and succeed, especially with targets who don't believe that my Master and the Creator are real.'

'What about those who do believe?' said Jonah.

'Vilde chooses his cleverest spirits and strongest demons to attack my Master's followers. They have to go through a different portal, which takes them to the Third Heaven, the place where they usually have to fight me and any of the other warrior angels that I command to join me.'

'So, these human followers never get tested then, if your angels do all the fighting for them?'

'My angels are the best fighting warriors ever created, but the fallen, evil angels that they fight gain extra strength from the choices, actions and thoughts of human sin.' Halecim explained.

'Remind me what sin is again?' Jonah was not sure if he had ever had this explained to him before but knew it was important to understand.

'Sin is anything that you do, say, or think that is against the Creator's standards of perfection. It causes a break in a human's relationship with the Creator. That is why his enemies have a strategy that encourages people to sin. The battles that my angels have are intense, and we can only win each fight if the human followers of my Master choose to fight with us. If a believer resists the temptation to do wrong, they weaken the power of the dark angels. That helps us win and sends them back to Hell, battered and bruised.'

Halecim seemed very dramatic as he explained all this, moving his arms around as though he was in the middle of one of the fierce battles he was describing.

'Why didn't you tell me all this before?' said Jonah, wishing he had understood earlier.

'It was not your time. Not then. Your unbelief had already given Theda the strength to attack you and that is why my Master sent me to protect you.'

Halecim saw that his young friend was trying to get to his feet but, every time Jonah tried, he found that he could not move his limbs properly. He felt disabled by a growing pain in his chest, a searing pain that crippled him and knocked him back to the ground. He stretched out his arm towards Halecim who grabbed it. Still Jonah collapsed to the ground. His protector watched him trying to get up and his face filled with concern.

'Jonah, that cluster of demons that has just wounded you has spent thousands of years gathering the deepest, darkest pain from all the humans who have allowed them to gain possession. When Legion touched you, it transferred some of that deep, human suffering into your soul. The wound you feel now is not your own. It is the pain of fallen souls who have never believed. I'm afraid there is nothing that I can do to help. I do not have the power or the authority to take away the consequences of their wrongdoings. All I can ask is that you believe in your head, and your heart, that this is not your pain. Try to be strong in overcoming it, until our mission is complete.'

Jonah thought about this for a moment, then nodded. He decided to try his best to ignore the pain and, with all his strength, make the effort to stand up again. This time it felt a little easier than before and he succeeded. Then Halecim made his way towards the main street, facing the rows of buildings. Jonah followed, watching as Halecim waited for a timely gap to pass through the regimental lines of spirits. Halecim navigated their way through three more lines of demons, moving swiftly between the burning structures, until they reached one that was smaller than the rest, about the size of a garden shed. This wooden shack was strangely different to the others in town. There were no lines of spirits heading towards it.

'This must be the one,' said Halecim. 'Only Vilde's specially selected demons are permitted to move around this part of the underworld and no-one is heading in this direction right now.'

They walked towards the shed and climbed the three short steps to the door. After Halecim reached out and slowly pushed it open, they stepped into a deserted room. As they did, Jonah recognised the same whirlwind he had felt in the deserted saloon.

'What is this?' he asked. 'I've seen it before.'

'It's the vortex that signals the entry to a darker world,' said Halecim. 'You may have noticed that as we pass through different Doorways, our journey is becoming more and more dangerous. But this is our mission, Jonah, our purpose now. It's the way we have to go, to rescue Beth.'

Just as Halecim finished speaking, and without warning, an unexpected force grabbed hold of them both and propelled them backwards into the portal and deep darkness. Within a few blinks of the eye, there was light again and Jonah saw they were standing on a boulder in the entrance of a cave. Looking out into the distance, from the mouth of the cave, Jonah could see more steaming hot sand in a desert that stretched endlessly before them. The cave, where they now stood, had a concoction of strange formations shaped from the molten rock pouring out of the portal, and twisted icicles protruded from the top of the entrance. Jonah was relieved they had landed on the boulder. A few centimetres to the right or left and they would have lost the skin off their feet in the scorching lava below.

'Things are going to get pretty scary now...so have this ready by your side and don't be afraid to use it,' said Halecim, handing Jonah the dagger which he had once trained with, in preparation for this time.

It felt so long ago, like a lifetime, since he had practiced his swordsman skills and Jonah was nervous about handling the weapon now. He knew he would probably have to use it to defend himself in battle. He grasped the handle with one hand and the sheath with the other and slowly pulled the dagger out of its holder. It was pristine, extremely well-polished, and made Jonah blink when the sparkling metal reflected a dazzling light into his eyes. He quickly pushed the blade back into its safe zone and then attached it around his waist, underneath his cloak. Halecim took the lead again and they continued their voyage, away from the cave entrance into another fierce sandstorm.

# 18

Nat walked through the door into his family's council flat, on the tenth floor of the high-rise block. It was a depressing place to be, with dirt and graffiti all over the walls, inside and out. Rubbish was left on the floors, mixed with used drug paraphernalia and disgusting looking liquids that smelt horrible. In fact, the whole place had the smell of an unclean public toilet and the appearance of a desolate warzone. Nat hated living in these flats, just like everyone else who lived there. At least, he thought, they all had one thing in common – none of them could escape.

Over the years, many people from other towns and cities had been parachuted in to try and 'change' the demographic of the estate and make it better. It was pointless, thought Nat. Nothing they did ever worked or lasted very long. Nobody understood what it was like to live in this poverty-stricken area, except those who had to live there because they had no choice. It was not just about the need for financial investment to improve the way it looked, or the desperate shortage of open spaces for children to develop, grow, and play together. The whole estate was in a mess.

Worse than the obvious scar of poverty that affected everyone on the estate was the lack of hope. Nat knew he was just one of many who felt trapped in a life of despair and misery, with no opportunities for things to change. He watched the adults on the estate spend their limited income on lottery cards, at the betting office or at bingo – anything that might give them the chance to strike lucky. He had never experienced anything other than this way of life and had hardly ever left the estate, other than a couple of class trips when he was in primary school. He never questioned whether things could change or be any different. He just accepted that this was his life. In his world, it was survival of the fittest.

On the streets, Nat was in control. Through working hard at the gym and the boxing ring, he had become the strongest gang leader in the area. But at home he felt tired and helpless. As he walked into his own personal hellhole, he began his usual routine of cooking, cleaning, stopping his sisters from fighting, changing his baby brother's nappy, and cleaning up after his mum whilst she lay asleep in her own vomit, surrounded by empty booze bottles.

Nat rolled up the sleeves of his hoodie and began his chores. Less than two hours later, he placed a meal of beans on toast on the table for his family. His sisters, aged seven and nine, had stopped arguing long enough to sit down for their tea and even his mum had made the effort to move from the settee to flop into a chair by the table, just six feet away. The kitchen was an extension of the living room – a small, poky room not big enough for all of them. Regardless, Nat had always fought for the family to share at least one meal together at the table. He was sitting there, helping baby Jack with his beans, when the front door opened.

In bounced Banksi. The second oldest son in the family, he was nicknamed Banksi from a very early age. It was because he liked to pretend that he was robbing banks – just like his father, who was in prison following an armed robbery. Now aged fifteen, Banksi's behaviour and career choices remained unchallenged. Who really cared? Crime was an acceptable career on this estate.

'What time do you call this?' asked Nat, as soon as his brother had closed the door.

'What you on about?'

'You know what time tea is, and you're late.'

'Calm down fam. It's not a problem,' said Banksi, laughing.

'Yes, it is. You know this is important,' said Nat sharply.

'It's only important to you, I don't give a –'

'Don't you dare talk like that in here,' interrupted Nat. 'Watch your mouth.'

'Yo, Bro, what's gotten into you?'

'Nothing,' snapped Nat. 'Just do as you're told and keep your mouth shut.'

The girls could see that Nat was becoming angry and they didn't want to be in trouble either, so they kept quiet and continued to eat. Their mum was still too drunk to know what was happening. She sat slouched in her chair, not responding to any of the conversation.

Banksi could feel the tension brewing and sat down, doing as he was told. Like everyone else on the estate, he feared Nat too. He looked up to him with the greatest respect and wanted to be just like him. Until recently. He had noticed the changes in Nat over the past few days and was finding it hard to deal with. He worried that Nat was becoming emotionally weak and he was not sure what to do about it.

They ate the meal in silence, which was unusual for Nat who usually kept the conversation going, wanting to know every single detail about everyone's day. Although he had a super-tough image to win respect on the streets, at home he had a much softer side. He would do anything for his family and for years played the role of Dad in the home. Nat's strong need to protect his family was one of the reasons that men did not stay with his Mum for very long. He had the ability to scare the living daylights out of them if they did anything wrong. Lately though, Nat had begun to wonder if his behaviour on the street was hypocritical. Was he contradicting what he stood for at home? Some of his victims were just like him – trying to protect their own families. Thinking about this, Nat felt a twinge of guilt.

The meal was finished. Chantelle and Cherrie cleared away the dishes. At least this was something his sisters could do to help. Nat used a baby-wipe to clean Jake's face and hands, then put his baby brother down on the playmat to have fun with his toys. Banksi was the only one who remained seated. Nat could tell something was on his younger brother's mind, so he waited for him to share it. Meanwhile, he kept thinking about the earlier experience in the alley and hoped the injured boy was alright. Nat had no idea how he was going to sort out Dan and the boys in the gang, but that was not as important to him as what happened to the boy they had just beaten up.

Suddenly, Banksi blurted it out. 'Nat, I've decided to join your gang.' He was grinning, as if he expected that this would bring a smile to his older brother's face and change the tense atmosphere in the room. He had shadowed Nat for years, inspired by him. Now, it was his chance to make Nat proud.

'No. Never. That's not going to happen,' said Nat, fiercely.

'Wh-what do you mean, I thought it would make you happy,' said Banksi, his voice shaking with shock and disappointment.

'Happy? No way. Today I saw my gang kick the hell out of an innocent lad, just because he wouldn't give them his phone.'

'Yeah but…that's what we do, isn't it? What's the problem?' Banksi was now upset and confused.

'Everything's the problem. Look at us. What have we become? Why do we have to use all this violence on innocent victims?'

'Because it's fun,' said Banksi.

'Fun!' said Nat, his voice full of anger.

'Yes fam, fun…'fact it's more than that. It's the only thing we've got,' said Banksi, shouting now.

Nat was dumbfounded at these words, realising how sad it was that this was true.

Banksi paused, then rose from his chair. As he headed for the front door, he said, 'Why have you changed Nat? Isn't life hard enough for us without you going all soft on us?'

Then he slammed the door behind him.

***

They were in their usual hangout, the bus shelter positioned near the off-licence. Nine lads, who aspired to be the 'top dogs' on the estate, just like Nat. They all thought they had what it took to be the toughest and rule the town with fear and power. They each believed the next step up to being the greatest was to follow Banksi, their leader, and learn from him. Their average age was about fourteen and, being a few months younger than their chief, were not as physically strong as Banksi. But their loyalty to him was second to none. He only had to say the word and these young rebels jumped to his orders.

Tonight, he arrived at the shelter looking angry and withdrawn, still in disbelief that Nat had rejected him so badly. He had spent his whole life longing to follow in the footsteps of his idol, always in awe and wonder of his older brother and the respect that he had earned through being a ruthless gangster. Now, Banksi sat down with his own gang and remained quiet. They did not know what to say or do. This was very unusual for their boss.

Bored and with nothing else to do, they followed the usual routine of sharing a few cigarettes, mixed with flakes of cannabis, between them – making a very weak 'joint'. None of them had any money. The only way to get some was to bully other kids, steal the occasional phone or wallet from a handbag, or smash car windows and grab whatever they could find. Most of them had very limited, if any, hopes and dreams for the future. They did not expect life to be more meaningful or exciting than the daily routine they faced each day. The only way things might change was if they were put in prison. Or manage to avoid being caught, rob a bank and be able to afford to drive around in a soft top BMW. That was the dream. That was why they followed Banksi. He wanted the big pay and he wanted to spend it, not like his old man who did get caught and was now doing a long stretch in prison.

Banksi had a plan. It was all laid out in front of him and he knew what steps to take, but it was a massive blow to his future not to get Nat's support. He had no idea what was wrong with his brother but he quickly realised he was now on his own. Sitting in the bus shelter, he made the decision that it was time for him to take over from Nat and stamp his own mark on the estate. He knew he would have to make a huge impact on the community to gain the respect of Nat's gang and to become their leader instead. He stood up and looked ahead, gazing over his self-declared territory and announced, 'Lads, we're going to war. This estate is ours. It's time for us to take over the streets. And we're going to begin our rule right now!'

The gang were really excited at this news, jubilant at the thought of being kings of the estate. With a few whoops of joy, they all stood together in unison, waiting in anticipation for what would happen next.

With his eyes on their first victim, Banksi walked straight into the off-licence and leaned over the counter. He grabbed the baseball bat that was hidden underneath (which everyone knew was kept there) and smashed the till to pieces. The lady behind the counter was petrified as the bat was hurled in her direction and the noise of the ravaging boys pierced the air with their frenzied shouts. As Banksi reached into the broken till to grab the money, the rest of the boys moved up and down the aisles knocking tins and boxes on the floor and smashing some bottles of alcohol, while opening and drinking others. They mindlessly wrecked the shop, scaring the shopkeeper so much that she cowered on the floor behind the counter, afraid for her life.

When they finished ransacking the place, the gang piled out of the shop together, scrambling over each other to get out the door, laughing and joking when two of them tripped on the pavement. Together they walked, skipped, and ran from the crime scene. On their way, a couple of them smashed the windows in the local bus stop and telephone box, using their feet and the newly acquired baseball bat. The sound of breaking glass fuelled their excitement and they searched for weapons and tools they could use to smash more glass windows as they passed. Cars, shops, houses, even the stained-glass windows of the old church, were smashed. They moved through the estate that night, wild and deranged.

# 19

It was exhausting, fighting their way through the sandstorm. As they neared the end of this grit hurricane, Jonah and Halecim noticed a bright red and orange glow in the distance. It was moving, slowly swaying in the wind, like a mirage. As they grew closer, they saw flames rising from the ground. Even closer, they recognised familiar shapes in the flickering fires; lines of tall trees, burning brightly. They were approaching a huge forest.

'What is it about burning wood in this place,' said Jonah. 'I mean, why is everything always on fire but nothing seems to disintegrate or disappear?'

He did not expect any answer, and he did not particularly want one either. It was just another mystery that he found himself wondering about. Halecim looked at him dubiously, wondering if he needed to answer this question, then carried on walking silently into the forest. They had not wandered far into the smouldering haze, warmed by the glowing flames, before Halecim signalled they should stop. He beckoned Jonah behind him, then reached inside his cloak to grab the handle of his sword. Jonah began to sweat with fear and the uncertainty of the moment as Halecim quietly led him forward, being careful to make as little noise as possible.

Treading carefully like elite Ninjas, they moved slowly towards a clearing about a hundred feet away from them. As Jonah concentrated on treading carefully, he could hear, above the noise of crackling wood, some voices in the clearing. Now, uncomfortably close, Halecim and Jonah stopped, crouched down behind a tree, and watched the strange display in front of them. Between the fire-red trees was a circular clearing where a group of ugly, scarred and disfigured demons sat around a makeshift table. Jonah counted there were nine of them; similar in form to the ugly creations that he had seen in the spirit town, but much older. Each figure bore the wounds of war and the disfigured limbs lost in battle. Jonah suspected that they may have done battle with Halecim and his angels at some point in time, and now wore the scars of those fights. Surprisingly, Jonah found he could understand most of the words they were speaking. He could not, however, recognise the names they called each other, as these sounded more like squeals, screeches and shrieks than actual words. He decided to give them his own names, identifying each by their physical appearance. There was Bumpy and Lumpy, Greasy and Three Toes, Boilie and Scabby, Gunky and Warty. The largest, and most ancient looking of them all, was Scar. He looked as if he had been in far more battles with sword wielding angels than any of the others.

As Jonah looked on, he noticed that they were playing a game with each other: one that involved nine sticks of different sizes and a big stone, about the size of a football. Each took it in turn to elevate the stone from the middle of the table, until it hovered at the eye level of the whole group. As it lingered in the air, they all drew sticks from a pile on the left of the table. Whoever had the shortest stick soon knew about it because the one controlling the stone sent it flying into their face, knocking them off their tree stump. As they crashed to the ground, the rest of the group laughed uncontrollably at the pain inflicted on the loser. He, or she, or whatever it was, then struggled up to return to their seat before the game started again. As Jonah watched this activity for a while, his focus began to shift towards the conversation the demons were having as they played this cruel game of chance.

'There are whispers of a war coming,' said Three Toes. He was the smallest demon in the group, although he showed no signs of inferiority, despite his size.

'Yeah, we know. Lord Vilde has created some new tools for us to use. Apparently, we're going to have to work harder to make the human scum think there's nothing to believe in,' said Lumpy. He was the most misshapen creature sitting there. His shoulders, elbows, knees and ankles had all been removed from their sockets and bizarrely repositioned further down his limbs.

'I prefer the old way of getting them…making them feel guilty when they've done something wrong…making them feel really worthless and useless…making them think nobody cares about them. These are the best ways to make them think the Creator either isn't there or isn't bothered about them,' said Greasy. He was covered in hair that was stuck to his skin with a slimy goo.

'Well. If we're all sharing our favourite tools for lying and deceiving the human scum, I quite like it when we pop up and scare them. Especially when they think we're one of their dead relatives. They must be so needy, to think that we're their family or even their dead pet, but they believe anything we say. It's a great laugh for me, and we don't get many chances to laugh down here, do we?' This came from Gunky, the funniest looking one of them all, due to the bubbles of mucus and phlegm dribbling out of his nose and ears

Most of the others nodded their heads and made grumbling noises in agreement. They all looked to Scar, the largest and scariest looking demon, who had four huge fangs coming out of his mouth, twice as many as all the others had. His limbs were covered in scars, including his gigantic blob of a nose where curly tufts of hair dangled from his oversized nostrils. He slowly stood to his feet and rested his scar infested arms on the make-do table. Looking around at all of them, he spoke with venom and hatred.

'Those pathetic, weak, pointless little human scum are our prey. Lord Vilde doesn't care about them, if they live or die, and he will do anything to stop their souls believing in the Creator. Our job is to stop them thinking they have any chance of being special or loved.' Scar almost retched when he spat out the word 'love,' as though it was a disease stuck in his throat. 'Whether they feel dirty, or guilty, or whether they sacrifice children to Lord Vilde is of no interest to our Master. You must remain focused on our task – to keep them doubting the Creator exists. You've all done endless tours of duty, spent many scum years with one target, constantly digging away at their mind and soul until it is beyond repair. You are privileged to be here in the lower underworld, close to our lord, because of your successful years of service.'

Scar stood up on his eight-toed, scar covered feet and began to walk slowly around the circle, feeling proud to be with his warriors. His words were turning into a motivational speech, rousing and stirring the ranks as though preparing for an imminent battle.

'We have all lost count of the souls we've condemned to an eternal life with us in Hell; those who we've convinced that our lord cares about them enough for them to become witches, satanic worshippers, fortune tellers or false prophets. We've used the old tools of false idols, crystal balls and tarot cards and added the new-age trappings of graphic sex, violence, drugs or anything that will feed their addictions. These humans are weak and easily tempted. We need to remember that. But...be careful. Be on your guard. As we teach and train our armies, we must continually remind them that even those who have the most pathetic and worthless lives, with nothing left to look forward to but death, even at the point we think we've won, they too can turn to the Creator. We may think their souls are beyond repair, but

He doesn't think that way. Remember there is nothing worse than spending fifty-plus years of hard work destroying a soul, only to lose them right at the end.'

The demon took a moment to stop and reflect, as if remembering the souls that had slipped away from him. 'It's time for us to get back to work. We have orders to focus our war on the inner weaknesses of each human scum, making each of them feel worthless, empty, guilty, pointless, unloved, helpless, dirty, bad, beyond repair, hopeless and much too sinful for forgiveness. We know our job has become easier recently, with all the new religious wars in the human's world. And, as their societies and families break down, the scum begin to accept evil as the norm. It's good for us that they feel let down by the hypocrisy of weak and washy religions that claim to know the Creator, even though they don't. But we can't rely on that. We need to work hard until the end of time. So, let's get to it, boys. Break over.'

The speech had done its job. The group looked truly motivated and ready to get back to work in their war on humanity. They all rose to their feet and headed off in a single line formation, heading towards the trees in the distance.

Jonah had listened intently, amazed at how many negative and nasty things in his world were used by these evil spirits and demons to attack humanity. He was not happy about humans being referred to as 'scum' all the time either, but he let that one go. Especially as Halecim continued to signal to him to be quiet and let the demons leave. He watched them disappear, one by one, through an invisible portal next to a large, burnt, oak tree.

As the last few demons waited impatiently for their turn, Gunky, still dribbling mucus, asked his leader, 'Where are you going today?'

'Into Lord Vilde's lair,' said Scar, 'to have some fun with a lowlife scum brought in by Theda.'

'That sounds like fun. Much better than my day. All I've got to do is train new recruits in how to use adult video games to get into the heads of children.' Gunky looked most displeased.

The demon in front of them, Warty, was the next to go through the portal, leaving the last two waiting for their turn.

'So, what terrible pain are you going to inflict on the scum?' asked Gunky, as if he wished he had the job.

'The scum human has already been tortured by Theda, but I'm going to start separating her nails from her fingers, then her fingers from her hands...'

Jonah began to feel queasy when the evil thing mentioned 'her'. Could they be talking about his mum?

'And then I'm going to separate every limb until she dies in pain, and her son will have no chance of saving her,' said Scar. As he began laughing a deep, horrible laugh, Jonah felt sick with fear. He was now convinced that this beast was going to hurt his mum.

As if reading his thoughts, Halecim reached out to grab Jonah before he did anything stupid. Too late!

Jonah was racing towards Scar and Gunky. Reaching under his cloak and firmly grabbing the handle of his dagger, he swept it out and aimed it at his targets. The demons heard the movement of crackling branches and saw the unfamiliar figure in their underworld...a human boy charging at them, waving a knife. They did not know whether to laugh at the pathetic object approaching them or prepare to fight him. Then a sudden look of horror crossed their faces when they saw Halecim, who had thrown off his gown, flying towards them at great speed. Grabbing their weapons, they held their swords in front of them, at arm's length, unable to move their feet, which seemed stuck to the ground as though cemented there.

Halecim gently pushed Jonah to the left, to aim his dagger in line with the smaller of his two opponents, whilst he aimed his own sword at Scar. Four pieces of strongly forged metal hit each other at precisely the same time.

Sparks flew everywhere as the swords struck in defensive holds and attacking thrusts. Jonah remembered everything he had been taught in the desert and, with the boxing footwork and body movements that Kyle taught him, he glided around Gunky like a professional swordsman. To the left, down to the right, swing around his head, jab in between defensive blocks. Jab and Jab. Jab again. Jonah was on fire with passion, not just the orange embers glowing on his trainers!

Halecim had a tougher fight with Scar but used his wings to protect himself against the evil blows. Swinging his much larger, more powerful sword, it did not take too many hits for the demon to lose his grip on the handle and watch his sword hurtle through the air and pierce the trunk of a burning tree. Halecim showed no mercy and thrust his sword into the demon's thick-skinned, hairy belly.

Jonah heard the squeal of pain as the large monster hit the ground and melted away. As he took his eyes off his own opponent for a second, it gave an opportunity for the little demon to drop his sword and run towards the portal entrance. Jonah turned and saw the evil thing running away but instinctively flipped his dagger into the air, caught it by the end of its blade, and threw it towards the fleeing demon. The high-pitched scream, when the blade went into Gunky's back, was almost deafening. As it landed, the ugly demon disintegrated into a pool of slime, leaving Jonah's weapon lying harmlessly on the ground. Jonah walked over to it, full of pride and feeling strong. He had just destroyed his first demon. Then, as he bent down to retrieve his dagger, he suddenly had a horrible thought. He turned to Halecim, not with a look of joy but with the terrible realisation of what he had just done.

'I've killed something... I'm...I'm a murderer,' he said, shaking with the shock.

Halecim put his wings away and picked up his cloak to cover himself up again. He reached out and took hold of Jonah's arms, which were still shaking and clammy with sweat, and led him through the trees, at lightning speed, away from the portal.

*** 

They quickly came to the edge of the burning forest, which opened onto the side of a lake – a lake that was on fire. It burned and bubbled with a strong smell of sulphur while the sand, that linked the trees to the water's edge, slowly curdled in puddles of acid that melted the grains with its heat. Rocks were exploding around the lake's edge, as they soaked up the toxic substance from the lake and grew excessively hot with the surrounding flames. It was not a safe place to be, but Halecim seemed to think there would be less chance of a demon popping up here than at the portal entrance. He knelt under the shade of a gigantic tree and, putting his hand on Jonah's shoulders, looked into his anxious eyes.

'Jonah, I know it must be hard thinking about what you've just done. You live in a world where taking another human's life is wrong. Your world was created with rules and boundaries for living in peace and harmony. It was meant to be that way and only the Creator has the right to give life and take it away. So, the consequences of a human killing another human is severe – physically, spiritually and emotionally.'

Jonah felt worse when Halecim started mentioning consequences but Halecim tightened his grip to reassure him and stop him moving away.

'Look around you, Jonah. This is not your world, this is not your planet Earth. It is not a place where humans can live. It's a world formed by a former angel, Vilde, once meant to serve the Creator, who rebelled and chose to rule this place instead,' said Halecim. 'This is a place filled with dark creatures that constantly choose to reject the Creator's love and offer of relationship. Believe me, that was not a human whose life you just took, or a human who had turned into an evil spirit – it doesn't work like that. That was a creature that chose to join forces with Vilde. A demonic being. When humans die, they do not join the battles of good against evil. That is our job. Millions and millions of angels were created at the beginning of time but far too many have followed the rebellion of Vilde. I lead the Creator's army against them. We are there to protect mankind and to fight against these despicable, abhorrent fallen angels who prefer to choose death over life.'

Jonah was comforted a little that he had not killed a fellow human, but still he had a few questions. 'Are you saying I'm fighting against fallen angels? Is that why they look so disfigured? I mean, none of them still have their wings, do they?

'That's right,' said Halecim. 'They lost their wings many thousands of years ago.'

'So, is it okay to kill these evil creatures? I don't need to feel guilty about it?'

'No, you don't. Guilt is a weapon that Vilde uses to make humans feel so bad that they think they can't ask for forgiveness. The Creator may hate the sinful things that humans do but still loves each person who does wrong more than they could ever imagine. He doesn't want to punish but to forgive…to get rid of anything that gets in the way of a loving relationship and carry on enjoying life.'

'So why don't you and your army just kill all the demons and get rid of the evil?'

'If only we could. But, because there is free will in your world, humans have an ability to choose what they do, right or wrong. If they choose wrong, then we must fight good and evil battles in the heavenly world to keep some order and balance in place. This is a spiritual war that will continue for some time. But one day, the war will be over.'

Halecim looked up towards the distant sky and Jonah saw a look of peace on the angel's face. It was clear he believed they were going to win the war.

'Then what are we doing wasting time here?' said Jonah, feeling surprisingly awake and energised. 'We have to fight some more demons and rescue my mum!'

Halecim beamed a massive smile, stood to his feet, stretched and flexed his muscles and started back into the forest, towards the portal. Jonah followed swiftly, hot on his heels.

# 20

Dan sat on the wall in the middle of the group, thinking about the last words spoken between him and Nat. They had been friends since they were five years old and he had always looked up to Nat. But now the summer nights were getting longer and lighter, and he and the rest of the gang were getting restless. Since their last episode with Nat, they had spent their time trying to figure out what they should do about their leader. Had he deserted them, or was he keeping his distance because he had other things occupying his attention? On this hot and stuffy evening, instead of the usual boisterous banter, or terrorising some unsuspecting prey, they sat around contemplating their future as a gang.

Dan always envied the power and respect that everyone showed Nat and he had hoped that one day he could take over the main leadership role. But he never thought it would happen like this. He had never argued with his best friend before but he struggled with the way Nat had reacted to the beating of the boy. Why did he suddenly care about his victim? Dan also felt guilty about the way he responded, shouting and barking at Nat. He hated challenging Nat about the way he was treating the gang these days but it had to be done. Now he felt angry and confused about the whole situation. Still, whatever feelings he had, there was a sense of urgency for him to get to grips with his emotions. Especially if he was going to be the one in charge of Nat's gang. He was the new boss. He was in control. As leader, he would have to keep up the macho act, without letting the others know how upset he was about falling out with Nat.

'What are we going to do about Nat then?' asked Jack, out of the blue.

'Eh?' Dan was still in deep thought, not really listening to the discussion around him.

The other boys, too scared to have this conversation, tried to ignore Jack but he wanted an answer. 'I said, what are we going to do about Nat?' he demanded, staring at Dan. 'You told him he was through with the gang if he left. Did you mean it?'

Dan thought carefully about his answer. He knew that if he showed signs of weakness and forgiveness, the others would not respect him as their new leader. Even though he'd thought about being the 'gaffer' for years, when it came down to it, he did not want to be the leader. Not as much as he wanted his friend back. He was confused and unsure, but a decision had to be made. He had to be strong so he chose loyalty to the gang – even though he knew it was the easy option.

'Nat has made up his mind. He made his choice...to go against us.' Dan jumped off the wall and stood tall as he turned to face the rest of his crew. 'So now he's gone, I'm the new leader,' he said as firmly as possible.

'Who put you in charge?' asked Stephan.

Dan was not expecting this challenge. 'I've always been second in command and it's only right that I now take the lead,' he said, slightly awkward about it.

Everything went quiet. Would anyone else challenge Dan's authority? Would there be a fight for supremacy?

Jack put his hand up and then quickly realised how silly he looked, as if he was at school. He put his hand quickly down again but still spoke like he thought he might be told off. 'I don't mind you being our leader Dan but…if we need to take a vote, that's okay with me.'

'A vote! A vote…what the hell do you think this is?' shouted Dan. 'This isn't some democracy or politics rubbish. This is my estate now. I'm the leader and if you don't like it, you can leave too.' He was furious. How dare they challenge him.

There were some shifty looks among the gang members as they were not sure if they were ready to accept Dan as their new leader. Except no-one else wanted the job. They simply wanted to have fun and do whatever they chose to do, to stop being bored. There was not much ambition between any of them. They had no great expectations or career dreams. For them, life was just about hanging around on the streets, trying to not let the boredom get too depressing. Most, if not all of them, had been told by parents and teachers that they were 'wasters' and 'good for nothing'. Their lives had become a reflection of the negative statements they kept hearing, repeatedly. Aware of this, Dan knew he needed to exert his authority immediately, to take control. He made the decision that the first person to wander into their alleyway that evening would be their next victim.

As soon as he had convinced himself that this was a good idea, a small elderly lady came tottering around the corner. She looked fragile and was slightly bent over, with her handbag held tightly over her left arm and an old-fashioned, wooden walking stick in her right hand. Dan could not believe his bad luck. Why did it have to be an old, weak lady? Why not a teenage lad who could give him a proper challenge? He wanted to let the woman walk past. He knew the right thing was to let her go. She was an innocent lady who did not deserve to be mistreated. But it was too late. He could not back down now. It was important to prove his strength and leadership. He could not go back on decisions. So, he moved forward and stood in front of the old lady.

She stopped when she peered and saw his feet before her on the pavement.

'Give me your bag.' Dan demanded.

The rest of the gang were shocked. Although they had a bad reputation in the community for being thugs, they had never preyed on anyone so old before. Yes, they would be happy to shout a few obscenities and nasty comments at a passing pensioner, but they all felt uneasy about going as far as mugging an old lady. It was embarrassing, especially when the woman tilted her head up towards Dan, who was at least three feet taller than her, and quietly asked him to repeat himself - she was having difficulties hearing. It was even quite comical, and some of the gang chuckled.

The inner turmoil that Dan was facing made him more determined to see this through. Shouting with anger, he repeated 'Give me your bag…you Old Hag.'

Clenching her bag, her arm tight against her body, the lady simply replied, 'No.'

Dan's rage quickly overpowered his conscience and he reached out to grab her bag. As he took hold of it, wrestling with the stubborn lady, she leaned towards him, gripping her bag for dear life, and soon tumbled over onto the concrete path. She cried out in pain as her fragile bones snapped.

This was not what Dan had planned. He began to panic and so did the rest of the gang. They all ran away, leaving the injured women lying on the pavement, alone.

*** 

Nat walked hurriedly into the gym, looking around to see where his new companion was. The boys and men, training hard, were spread around the room using a variety of apparatus and training equipment in the arena. A couple of the men had previously lived on the estate where Nat had spent his entire life, but most of them now lived in the more affluent parts of town. They kept well away from the tragic concentration of high-rise flats and poverty-stricken families on the estate. Most people only went to the estate if they had to. It had nothing to offer except a place to buy drugs, or somewhere to find a thief to steal a car for an insurance scam. Though, surprisingly, it had the best Chinese take-away in town!

Kyle was not in the main hall, so Nat raced around the community centre until he found him in his office. He was on his knees, facing the back wall.

'Kyle, are you okay?'

Kyle was not expecting anyone to disturb him and was taken aback for a moment as he turned and stood up. 'Yes, I'm fine. I was just…ah, I was just…well, I was just praying, to be honest.'

'Oh. Sorry to interrupt,' said Nat, unsure whether to stay or go. He decided to stay. 'It's an emergency,' he stuttered.

'What is?'

'Kyle, there are some terrible things going on in the estate and I don't know what to do about them. It's getting out of hand.'

'Tell me what's happening,' said Kyle, pointing to an empty chair the other side of his desk.

After they both took a seat, Nat continued, 'I've upset everyone with my recent decisions. Trying to change who I am. I mean, I want to change. But my family and friends don't like it. They don't understand.'

'Change is a very scary thing, especially for people who don't know any other way of life,' said Kyle.

'But they are taking it really bad.'

'Who is?'

'Banksi and Dan. I've just been informed that Banksi's raised his own army of young guns, just kids…thirteen, fourteen-year olds, following him around the estate. They're smashing windows, running into shops and stealing stuff. Then Dan has put an old lady in hospital. All because of me.'

'Why?' Kyle was confused about why Banksi and Dan would respond to Nat's choices in this way.

'Well, apparently, I heard Dan has taken over my role as leader and wants to stamp his mark on our gang. He started by robbing an old defenceless lady, who decided to fight back. And then Banksi…well, he's always looked up to me and now I think he's trying to copy me…or what I used to be like.'

'I see. So, what are you going to do about it?'

Nat sat for a moment, not sure that he had an answer. Was it his fault that this was happening? Could he stop the trouble? 'Is it my responsibility to change what the others are doing?' he asked.

'Nat, it's about choices. You made a choice to stop the violence and try to change the atmosphere on the estate. But I told you at the beginning that this would not be easy. It's probably going to get worse before it gets any better. You've chosen to step away from an evil lifestyle and the people who once looked up to you don't know how to take it. They are probably confused. Nothing prepared them for this moment. It sounds like Dan and Banksi are returning to the natural human instinct of fighting for survival. It's up to you to show them that they too can have a choice. They can choose good rather than evil.'

'But how do I show them that?' asked Nat.

'From within.'

'Within what?' Nat was confused.

'From within the battlefield,' said Kyle.

Nat realised that Kyle was right and thought about his responsibility to his best friend and his brother. He understood life on the street. He knew how to fight and how to survive, but he also knew how to lead. He would have to make it his purpose, his task, to save them both by tackling them in the world he knew best, not leaving them to fend for themselves. He stood up and so did Kyle, who reached out and put his hand on his young friend's shoulder.

'I'm with you all the way Nat. We'll do this together.'

Nat managed a small smile and then they both made their way out of the centre.

# 21

Standing at the portal entrance, Jonah and Halecim both knew this would be their final plunge into the depths of Vilde's lair. They were about to face their toughest battle. Taking hold of their swords, they stepped into the darkness and were whisked away through the long corridors of the portal. Within milliseconds, they arrived at the black hole of the portal exit and stepped out into the worst place that has ever existed.

On either side of the doorway, two demon warriors stood to attention. They were large hairy beasts with bent backs, thick and crooked legs, and arms covered in boils and scars. No-one ever came through this portal unless they were invited.

Until now. It was clearly a shock for the demons when they saw Halecim and Jonah suddenly appear in front of them. The look of horror and surprise was evident on their disfigured faces as they fumbled around for their primitive weapons. Too late. Before they could raise their spears or shields, Halecim and Jonah had thrust their swords into the stomachs of each demon and stood, in solemn silence, as these abhorrent creatures melted away into nothingness.

With a surge of relief, Jonah looked around to see where they were. He was quite surprised to see that they had arrived very near the top of a huge mountain and were balanced on a small ledge. He could see for miles below and caught a glimpse of the massive army of demonic beings camped at the foot of the mountain, far too many to count. These were the fallen angels Halecim had told him about. Although they were once beautiful creatures, made in majestic form with glistening white wings and perfectly formed muscular bodies, like Halecim, now they were only dark malformations of their former self. It seemed they could still hover over the ground and move quickly but there were no signs of wings, or anything white. They were in an army camp, but they seemed to lack structure; no training areas for weapons practice, no ordered queues waiting for food, nothing that Jonah expected to see in a camp waiting for battle.

'It doesn't look very organised down there,' said Jonah.

'No. There is only chaos and immorality in this place,' said Halecim. 'No-one shares anything or works as a team. They are all trying to preserve their own pathetic lives and survive. They don't need to train, anyway. They are all very accomplished at being evil. They've had many years of practice.'

Fortunately, the armed companions did not need to walk down the mountain towards the camp. Their final journey was into the deep crevices and hidden caverns of the mountain. Halecim led the way, whilst Jonah took a final glimpse at the evil chaos below before turning to follow his friend. The entrance to the mountain was dark, cold and very wet. Water dripped from the rocks above their heads and covered every inch of the narrow passageways.

It was the first time that Jonah had felt chilly since entering the dark underworld. At least it was a change from the burning sensations of steaming rocks and flames he had so far experienced. The entrance to the crevice was low at first but it was not long before it spread open to reveal a gigantic cavern, so huge it was as though the whole mountain was hollow or had been gutted to create a fortified arena. There were steps leading around the side of the cavern - thin, slippery, and dangerous steps with no handrails to cling to.

Concerned for Jonah's safety, Halecim walked slowly as Jonah followed carefully. The steps were covered in black ice and wet with moss and slime, so extreme care was needed. A few slips, trips, and close calls later they reached a platform, several hundred feet below the entrance. It was a creaky wooden construction, barely strong enough for a giant angel and a teenager to be standing on at the same time. Looking around to see where they could go next, Jonah's right foot slipped off the edge. Halecim grabbed his arm and pulled Jonah back swiftly, pushing him towards the wall to save him from falling into the belly of the mountain, a thousand feet below.

Suddenly, Jonah disappeared.

'Where's he gone?' Halecim said to himself, confused by this apparent vanishing act.

A few moments later, a head poked out through the wall of rock.

'This is an illusion, Halecim. There isn't any rock here,' said Jonah, laughing. 'Though I did land with a thump when you threw me into the wall. But thank you for saving me, anyway.'

Halecim frowned and then walked through the wall (that was not a wall) to meet Jonah on the other side. He scanned their territory to plan the way they should go. 'We need to be careful, Jonah. I didn't expect there would be such tricks and illusions here, just the demon warriors. Be aware, things may not be as they appear on the surface. You must judge everything by what you have already learnt on your journey. Think of what the Storyteller would say and do in each situation, not what your instincts tell you.'

Jonah was concerned. He had been preparing for a physical battle, a fight to the death maybe. But he was never strong in a mental or emotional struggle. He began to feel weak again and was even more thankful that his guardian angel was still with him.

The other side of the illusory wall had three identical tunnel entrances. Another trick. Which was the right path to take? Halecim contemplated for a few seconds and then decided to take the middle tunnel. The walkway was not very big and the giant warrior filled the whole space.

As he walked along, he had to stoop and lower his head to his chest. The top of his wings scraped the ceiling, occasionally knocking small pieces of loose rock and ice onto Jonah, who was walking closely behind him. It became very dark as the light from the mountainside entrance began to fade, and Jonah kept apologising for bumping into Halecim.

Soon they reached an opening, which pleased them both. The cavern before them felt colder than anywhere they had been before. The water running down the walls had turned into twisted icicles, some over ten feet long and three feet wide, hanging from the rocks above and suspended only inches from the ground. The dim glow from the yellow-white ice gave some light, allowing Jonah and Halecim to distinguish the contours and shapes of the cavern.

This time Jonah went first, carefully moving between the icicles. There was not much space between the obstacles and, within a short while, the distance between the two companions had grown greater. Jonah, being smaller in build, slipped through the suspended icicles easily but his friend and protector struggled to push through and spent his efforts focused on trying not to break the ice. When he looked up, he was surprised to see that his companion was now quite far ahead.

Jonah had reached a point where the icicles protruded upwards from the ground rather than hanging from above. Either that or the cave had been turned upside down! Was it an illusion? The icicles seemed more transparent and reflective than the frosted icicles at the beginning of their journey. He caught a glimpse of himself in one of the ice-mirrors and stopped to see what he looked like. Everything looked different. His clothes had changed. They were not what he knew he was wearing that day, so it could not be an actual reflection.

As Jonah stared deeper into the ice-mirror, he suddenly saw himself stealing a bar of chocolate from the sweet shop on his estate. He must have been only about eight years old but he vividly remembered doing it. Then he saw himself in front of his English teacher, telling her his homework had been eaten by his dog, although he had not done that piece of homework and did not have a dog. 'It was only a little white lie,' he thought.

The images kept appearing before his eyes, showing countless other memories of his life...whenever he had done, thought, or said, something bad. He remembered that he had not even thought he was doing anything wrong at the time. Now, he was painfully aware of all the countless times he'd sworn, the lies and deception he'd used to get himself out of trouble, the hatred and unforgiveness towards his dad for leaving them, the jealousy of his friends who still had fathers living with them, and the argumentative and cruel words he spoke to his mum.

Staring into his past like this, seeing all his wrongdoings, Jonah felt terrible. His emotions ran high with fear and guilt. He felt worthless and dirty all over. He began to hear the cries and screams of the people he had hurt and upset in the past. He tried to block their voices out of his ears by pressing his palms tightly over his ears but the sounds pierced through the skin and bones on his hands and into his eardrums. The searing pain, both physically in his ears, and emotionally in his soul, brought him to his knees. The tears rolled down his cheeks. He had never felt so low and wicked at any point in his entire life. His erratic breaths froze in the arctic climate and clouded the smooth surface of the ice- mirror in front of him. He was so consumed in the mire and mess of his despair that he did not feel his protector's hand on his shoulder, or the strong arms lifting him up off the ground.

Halecim knew very well what had just happened to Jonah and wanted to get him out of the cave as quickly as possible. Holding his friend tightly, he moved quickly, darting in and out of the frozen obstacles in his way, to find the exit. Once he squeezed them through the tight hole at the far end of the cave, he carried Jonah back through the inner tunnels of the mountain until he found a place to stop and put him down.

Although his tears had dried, Jonah was still bleary-eyed with shock. He stared with a vacant look into the distance, seemingly unaware of his rescuer.

'Jonah. Jonah, can you hear me?' Halecim gently shook his friend to try and grab his attention.

Slowly, Jonah began to recognise his personal angel. He could not speak.

'This is one of the most effective weapons that Vilde uses,' said Halecim. 'He loves to keep reminding you of all the things you've done wrong and the mistakes you've made. He has no better form of attack than making you believe you're not worthy to be in the presence of the Creator, not able to apologise for your wrongdoings or seek forgiveness. Vilde tells lies like no other. He tells you that you are evil, that you have no good in you. But that is a lie.'

Halecim's voice trembled with anger as he described the most subtle and deadly weapons of self-destruction. He paused for a moment to catch his breath, then continued, 'You must not believe that you are worthless. You were created to be loved – to be in a positive, caring relationship with the Creator.'

'No. All that I saw just now was true. That was really my life, it's not a lie,' said Jonah, miserable.

'I'm not saying what you saw was a lie. I'm saying Vilde whispers lies that make you believe you're not good enough to be in the presence of the Creator. And that's not true. I can't explain it all just now, but you need to believe me.'

Halecim seemed frustrated that he could not fully explain what he was trying to say. He tried to help Jonah snap out of his self-pitying trance by changing his tactics. 'Jonah, whatever has just happened, you need to put it aside. It's in the past and we need to focus on the present – saving your mum. That's what we're here for.' He stood quickly to his feet, ready to go, encouraging Jonah to move too.

It worked.

Jonah pushed himself to his feet and took a deep breath. Halecim was right. He had to think about his mum now, not wallow in events from the past. He followed his protector through the tunnels as they moved downhill, getting ever closer to the depths of the mountain and to Vilde's torturous chamber.

# 22

The evening was soon upon them as Nat and Kyle walked out of the fitness centre. There was a gentle breeze in the air and the night was still light with the blood-orange glow from the setting sun and the haze from a few remaining street lamps that had not been vandalised. There was very little movement around the empty streets and they only saw one or two people as they walked around the estate.

A car pulled up outside the Chinese take-away and the round-faced, obese driver stared in disappointment at the 'Closed' sign on the door. It was not the usual yellow printed sign that hung in the window, but a hastily scribbled note sellotaped to the door that read: 'Closed due to vandalism.' The man drove away in a hurry.

Nat knew something was wrong. The streets were too quiet. Rumours had spread quickly around the estate that there would be trouble tonight. Most people were too afraid to go out. They stayed locked away in their own homes, frightened of what was to come. There were plenty of signs of Banksi's earlier vandalism: shop windows were boarded up, piles of splintered glass lay on the pavements at every bus stop and phone box window that had been smashed to pieces. It would stay that way.

The Town Council were never very quick to repair damage on the estate. There was a general feeling that, if the residents did not unite and complain together, the elected officials could simply ignore the isolated reports of a failure in their service to the estate. They were right. There was no unity or community spirit in this disadvantaged part of town; nothing to bring the people together, nothing they had in common. All that united them was pain and poverty. Like a self-contained prison, this small estate dealt with its own problems and difficulties, using the only tools it had – violence and aggression. The alleyway where Nat had spent most of his empty days was deserted. The usual faces that graced these pavements and their loud, silly laughter was absent. It was like a ghost town.

Nat and Kyle sat on the alley wall, listening to the eerie silence and waiting to see what the night ahead would bring. They did not have to wait too long before signs of chaos emerged. A firework whizzed and sizzled up into the air, a couple of streets away from where they sat. A huge bang followed as the rocket exploded and then plunged to earth. Several other fireworks followed in quick succession as Nat and Kyle jumped off the wall and headed in the general direction of the lights and noise. They walked quickly, almost running towards the centre of the estate. Although fireworks were not normally associated with a riot, both knew that this was the first warning sign. It was a call to arms for all the gang members.

A small grassy area, between the high-rise blocks and smaller three-storey flats, was usually filled with small children kicking a ball around. Now, there were no children to be seen. Instead, a group of teenagers gathered – wearing baggy jeans, hoodies, and red bandanas to hide their faces and identity. No-one seemed excited by the noises or pretty colours of the exploding fireworks. They were waiting for something far more dangerous to happen.

As Nat and Kyle turned the corner from the alleyway into the grassy square, an old car exploded in front of them. It was thrown over six feet up into the air before it smashed back down on the road in a burning heap. The force of the explosion lifted Nat and Kyle off their feet and flipped them backwards onto the pavement. Window curtains twitched as people all around the square peeped out to see what was happening. One solitary door opened as the owner of the car came running out, to see who had just blown up his precious motor. The retired, balding man did not make it far down his short, well-kept, path before the car that was parked next to his also exploded in the same manner. The elderly gentleman did not have the strength to resist the forceful explosion. It sent him flying back to where he came from, straight into his hallway and onto his backside.

Nat and Kyle had just recovered from the first blast when the second one knocked them down again. They watched in horror as a third, fourth and fifth car in the parking area began to explode, one at a time. It was like watching something out of a Hollywood blockbuster movie (with a massive budget for special effects). These were controlled explosions that any stunt man would have been proud of. So, who was responsible for this explosive work of art? However deadly and dangerous this act of vandalism threatened to be, it was spectacular.

The orchestrator was delighted with his achievement as he stood and watched the show. While the cars finished exploding, the smoke and dust settled and the gang of awestruck young people clapped and cheered their leader. Banksi was thrilled with the effects of his deadly stunt and revelled in the accolades of his followers until he saw, through the evaporating smoke and diminishing flames, Nat and Kyle walking straight towards him.

'What the hell have you done?' Nat shouted.

Banksi was not happy to have his moment of victory spoiled by his goody-goody brother. Who did Nat think he was? As if a few good deeds now could change every bad thing he had done in the past.

'That's right brother. Welcome to Hell.' Banksi raised his arms and opened his hands as he twirled around, suggesting that all around him was home to the devil.

'What are you on about?' said Nat. 'What have you done here?'

'Just a little trick I've learned off my old man. We needed something to talk about during the prison visits,' said Banksi with a big grin on his face. He was proud as punch that his trick had worked. This was just the start of a wild night of fun and terror.

'That's enough,' said Nat, reaching out and grabbing Banksi's arm. 'I'm taking you home.'

'Gerr-off me,' said Banksi, enraged. He shook his arms and body wildly to rid himself of his brother's grip.

His little followers tried to move in closer to defend their beloved leader but when Kyle stood in front of them, they stopped in their tracks. None of them wanted to be beaten senseless by the town's famous boxing champion.

Banksi broke free from his brother's grip and quickly skipped backwards to get out of the way. 'You don't own this town anymore, Nat. It's mine, all mine. There's nothing you can do about it.'

Nat could hardly believe what he was hearing. 'This isn't a game Banksi. There are lives at stake. Your stupid little stunt tonight could have killed someone.'

Banksi's triumphant facial expression changed dramatically to a bitter sneer. 'You don't get it, do you? I've spent my life trying to be just like you. You were my idol. You had power, strength, respect. You were feared by everyone on the estate. That's what I longed for too. What's happened to you, Nat? You've become weak and pathetic, the opposite of what you used to be. You've hurt me, bro. You've abandoned me. Let me down. Now it's my turn to rule.' As he turned and ran away, he whistled for his hounds to follow. The noise they made was like wild dogs barking, or wolves howling. They left the burning wrecks of cars and raced towards their leader.

All Nat could do was stand and watch as his younger brother, whom he loved dearly, led his little gang into more rampaging. There was no use chasing after him, Nat knew that.

Meanwhile, Kyle had gone over to the old man who had been thrown to the ground, to make sure he was not too badly hurt by the blast. Nat joined him, knowing that soon they would have to plan their next move. They had to stop this violence.

*\*\*\**

On the other side of the estate, Dan and his gang were preparing for their own battle. They had heard the rumours that Banksi was causing havoc and they knew that they had to challenge him, to maintain their status as the top thugs on the estate. There was no way on earth that they were going to take orders from kids much younger than themselves, so this was a battle they were prepared to fight.

They met inside their headquarters – the garage plot which had become their 'cotch'. This was a place they could normally chill out on a couple of settees, with a fridge full of lager. Tonight, things were different. They all lined up to choose their preferred weapon for the fight ahead. Two of them chose wooden bats, one of them grabbed a steel bar, and all armed themselves with knives and knuckle dusters. They did not want to take any chances and tooled up, ready to claim their rightful place on the estate. Dan checked each member of his gang was carrying a suitable weapon and then led them out of the cotch, towards the rising smoke of the burning cars. Crackling and sizzling noises and the thick smell of sulphur from the burning metal filled the air. Then came a new sound – the shattering and splintering of glass, not from the cars but from windows being smashed a few streets away.

'That's where they must be now...over in that direction,' said Dan, pointing.

His gang began to run towards the sounds of broken glass but stopped, surprised, to see a familiar figure walking towards them.

'What do you want?' said Dan, greeting Nat in a sullen and unwelcoming tone.

'I want to reason with you, Dan. Tell you, all of you, that there's a better way than this. Why don't you join me?' Nat looked around the group and offered his raised hands to symbolise that he would welcome any of them back with open arms.

'Too late. You've had your day, Nat. You deserted us, remember? You've made your choice, so leave us to make ours,' said Dan, furious at this gesture.

Although some of the others in the group wanted to discuss Nat's offer, they knew they must walk away from their former master to follow Dan.

Nat was bitterly disappointed at this response and stared, bleakly, at the pavement. He was unsure what to do next.

'Be patient, Nat. This isn't easy for them either,' said Kyle, quietly. 'Think how tough it's been for you to change your lifestyle. You made the transformation because you were ready to, not because someone else asked you to.'

Nat lifted his chin and thought about how he would feel if someone had forced him to change before he was ready. 'Okay. I get it. This is going to be harder than I thought. But I can't stop now.'

Kyle nodded, patting Nat on the back, and then they both continued in the direction of the two gangs, walking towards the sounds of chaos.

***

Banksi was leading his followers on a rampage of terror around the estate, smashing anything made of glass, vandalising anything they could find – pulling up plants, denting cars with baseball bats, spraying vulgar words over shop doors and house walls with paint-spray. They were making a real mess and no-one was prepared to stop them. Even the police did not try to respond to the cries for help. After an hour of treacherous carnage, the young boys ran out of energy and became tired.

They stopped to rest on a small grassy area on the edge of the estate. They opened the sweets and drinks that they had stolen from the newsagents, whilst ruining hundreds of pounds of the owner's stock. They felt content with their work, enjoying the sounds of crying and shouts of anger echoing around the estate from all the victims they had left behind. The gang laughed and joked as they boasted about their exploits and what they had just achieved. Banksi was the only one standing, positioning himself at the centre of them all so that his adoring followers could look up and see him. He stood with his hands in his pockets, smugly admiring his work.

Banksi's expression soon changed when he saw his brother's gang turn the corner and head straight towards them. He was not sure who was leading the gang, or if the rumours of Nat's return were true, so he darted a quick look at each person heading in his direction, just to make sure. He sighed with relief when he realised Nat was not among them.

'What do you think you are doing to my estate?' Dan shouted at Banksi.

'Oh, but this isn't your estate, Dan. It's mine,' said Banksi, still defiant.

Dan and his posse stood in front of the younger kids, towering over them all, even though everyone was now standing.

'That's where you're wrong, little boy. It's time for you to run home to Mummy and play.'

'I am playing Dan. This is fun. And if anyone is acting like a child, it's the one who's too weak to fight a bloke and instead takes on an old granny,' said Banksi. He led his crew in hysterical laughter at the thought of Dan beating up the old-age pensioner.

Dan's embarrassment was intense. Seething with rage, he leapt towards his opponent and smacked him in the mouth. He knocked Banksi off his guard and sent him tumbling backwards as he hit the pavement hard.

No-one else expected this to happen. Over the past few days, Dan had become an aggressive, almost deranged person, with no self-control or common sense. It seemed his only strategy for making it as gang leader was to use violence, at any cost.

Dan stood over Banksi, thrusting out a clenched fist. 'Your place, boy, is under me. Remember that.'

No one challenged Dan.

No one protected Banksi or came to his rescue.

Dan felt good. In fact, he felt invincible. He was the proven leader of the gang. He was the ruler of the estate. It felt awesome. He stood up and walked away from his victim, feeling very pleased with himself.

Nat and Kyle stood watching the events unfold from a distance. They knew they could not barge in and break things up. Neither of the two lads at the centre of the row had any time for Nat – his choices had hurt them both.

Kyle had already explained to Nat that some things in life need to be played out to the end. Using the analogy of a boxing match, he explained how a referee only intervenes when the fighters are breaking the rules, or there is a high risk of serious injury. A punch in the mouth was not enough to justify jumping in to save the day. Even though it was difficult for Nat to see his brother and his best friend fight, he needed to wait.

However, when Nat spotted a six-inch blade shining in the light of the streetlamp, he had to shout out.

'Banksi. Stop.'

Banksi had whisked the knife from his back pocket and was raising it towards his intended target. There was no way he was going to let Dan get away with embarrassing and hitting him. Weapons were not a normal feature of Banksi's gang's tactics (they were scary enough without any need for deadly tools) but he had discussed his plan for estate dominance with his dad in prison. After many conversations on the subject, his father's influence made Banksi think it was okay to choose to carry a weapon. Now, he was going to use it.

Kyle moved much quicker than Nat but not fast enough to stop the blade piercing Dan's clothes, then his skin, before it finally punctured his lung. As Dan collapsed, Kyle caught him in his arms and they landed together on the road.

Onlookers from both gangs could hardly believe the events unfolding before their eyes. One of Dan's gang, Jack, may not have agreed with his leader that evening but he was still a loyal follower and was not going to let Banksi get away with this horrific act. He plunged towards him with a thunderous war cry. The rest of Dan's gang followed Jack and ran at the enemy, fists and knives flying in all directions.

They met their match. The younger gang may have been smaller physically but they outnumbered the older group by two to one and, as Banksi had also ordered his troops to carry weapons, injuries were inflicted heavily on both sides. It was a quick and vicious fight.

While Kyle kept pressure on the knife wound, holding his hand firmly over Dan's blood-soaked clothes, only Nat was available to try and referee the anarchy. Nat was still the strongest, by a long way, and he managed to pull the younger kids off his friends and throw them onto the pavement. As each one came crashing down on the concrete, they cried out in agony. Although they carried a wide variety of weapons between them, they were clever enough to know that challenging Nat would end in deep, long-lasting trouble for them all.

As Nat looked at them threateningly, each member of the two gangs decided to leave the struggle and hobble away to nurse their wounds. Now that their leaders were injured, they did not want to hang around the streets anymore. Their cries and moans began to quieten down as, one by one, they walked away.

Suddenly, the focus of Nat's attention moved from the last couple of scrapping lads towards the familiar voice of his younger brother.

'Nat, help me,' cried Banksi, out in obvious pain. He was lying on the road, near to Kyle and Dan, scrunched up in the foetal position and clutching his stomach. Nat moved towards him quickly and, as he parted his hands, he saw the same knife that had pierced Dan's back was now stuck in Banksi's stomach.

'Oh no... No!'

Frantically, Nat tried to stop the bleeding. 'What have I done?' he kept shouting. 'It's my fault...all my fault.'

Kyle did not have any words to console him as they both knelt over the wounded youngsters. How could they keep these two gang leaders from bleeding to death? Kyle reached across to Nat and grabbed his arm tightly.

Then something very strange began to happen. As all four held on to each other, the atmosphere began to change around them. A soft breeze pressed hard on their faces and they each felt themselves suddenly rising above the pavement – blown off their feet at a speed that seemed to defy the laws of gravity. The beckoning graveyard of the streets was fast disappearing as forces beyond their control whisked them up and away, through the cold night air to a place far, far away.

# 23

When Jonah and Halecim finally reached the edge of Vilde's central lair, they stood silently scanning the vast cavern trying to see who, or what, was ahead of them. They had reached the core of the dark and evil underworld, where goodness and love had been extinguished. It had probably never been present in this fire-burning, ice-freezing pit of despair. Nothing good had ever entered this world before and both Jonah and Halecim felt nervous and uneasy as the crushing pressure of the demonic, sinful atmosphere surrounded them. Although they were in the heart of the main cave, they could not see as far as the central dungeon where Halecim expected Beth to be. All they could see was a huge, open void. Burnt, black rocks and sandstone blocks created the walls and turrets of a castle fortress in the middle of a massive arena.

On their journey, Halecim had told Jonah that Vilde was consumed with a deep craving - the desire to be the most powerful creature in the whole of the universe, the heavens and the underworld. Standing here now, Jonah could see that Vilde had no interest in material possessions. The emptiness of his 'palace' revealed this clearly. All that decorated the bleak walls were grotesque

carvings that depicted stories of Vilde's many victories –
the souls he had ruined and destroyed ever since time and
creation began. The artistry was twisted but quite brilliant,
though Jonah was not here to admire the carvings. He
was here to rescue his mum. He followed Halecim quietly
and slowly, as they both crept closer and closer towards
the centre of the lair.

***

The demon-guards had been taunting Beth again, circling
her slowly but purposefully, calling her cruel names and
mocking her when she cried. Now they had left her alone
for a few minutes. Exhausted by the taunts and torments,
she crouched in the hot ash and tried to rest her tortured
mind for a moment but gradually became aware of a
strange smell. For several days, Beth had suffered the
stench of burning lava rock, sulphuric acid, and charcoal
mixed with stale sweat. But this smell was different. It
was the smell of humans.

As Beth slowly and painfully lifted her head, she saw a
curl of mist begin to appear about six metres in front of
her. The wispy smoke swirled around like a candyfloss
getting larger and larger, moving swiftly in a clockwise
direction. Beth's eyes burned as she strained to peer
through the mist to see what would be revealed when the
swirling disappeared and she could just make out some
darker, shadowy objects in the background.

In the distance, unseen by Beth, Halecim and Jonah
were watching from the shadows. Jonah could see his

253

mum tied to the pole, and it made his heart pound. He wanted to rush towards her but Halecim put a restraining hand on his shoulders. He pointed at the mysterious whirling mass, now growing stronger in shape and form, as it arrived only a few metres in front of Beth and came to a halt.

Of all the things that Jonah had experienced since travelling to the underworld, none was more surprising than this. There, emerging from the wisps of smoke, were Kyle and three of the lads who lived on his estate.

Nat looked really surprised as he sat cross legged on the ground. Dan and Banksi were resting against his arms, both bleeding badly from knife wounds that each of them had sustained during their fight on earth. They seemed barely conscious. Meanwhile, Kyle was on his feet. He seemed less surprised to be here but seemed to be looking for something, or someone, in the dim and dusky light of the lair.

'Help me. Please help me,' Beth suddenly cried out.

At this, Kyle and Nat turned their heads and were shocked to see Jonah's mum tied to a stake, held captive in such an inhumane way. Nat was in no position to help Beth at this moment. He was still trying desperately to put as much pressure as he could on the stab wounds of his best friend and his brother as they lay, squashed together, on his lap. He clung to them tightly.

It was Kyle who slowly walked towards Beth, as if he was going to try and set her free but, after only a few steps, he was suddenly confronted by the arrival of the demon-guards returning to their prisoner. They hissed with fury that four imposters had infiltrated the highest security area of Vilde's lair. How could they have done this without any warning or alarms being sounded?

They began to attack at once, flying at Kyle and brushing against his clothes as they darted forwards and backwards with extreme speed. He tried to push them away with his hands but they were too fast for him. One of the evil beings pushed him backwards and he tripped over Nat and landed hard on the slimy ground.

Beth's head dropped again as the chance of any immediate rescue faded. It increased her sense of hopelessness.

Kyle was not amused. He stood to his feet and was about to lunge at the ugly beasts again.

'Kyle, wait.'

Kyle turned, startled. Then his face broke into a broad smile when he saw who was calling him. He made a salute in the direction of Halecim and stood to attention.

Jonah watched, confused by what had just happened. He could not understand how Kyle, or any of the lads from the estate, had arrived in this dark place. How did Kyle know Halecim? Had they discovered the Doorway? Was the portal breaking down? Is that how they came here? So many questions. He lurched forwards, ready to run towards Kyle.

Halecim held him back. 'Jonah, stop.'

'But...'

'We are going to have to fight these demons first, so we can release your mum. You need to focus.'

There was so much that Jonah had been through on his recent journeys that he had learnt when to listen, when to challenge, and when to obey. Now, he joined his brave warrior friend as they pulled their swords from their sheaths and headed towards the demons, ready for battle.

'Jonah,' shouted Nat, in complete surprise that the boy who had stood up to him and his gang, who had challenged everything he stood for, was now walking towards him with a seven-foot winged man, wielding a sword.

Beth looked up with a jolt. It was incredible to hear her son's name uttered in this terrible place but now she could see him coming towards her. How much he had changed. No longer was Jonah the stroppy boy who walked around hunched and sulky because he was told to tidy his room. Here he was, standing tall and strong, a young man on a mission to save her. Despite this being the worst place that she would ever want him to come, she was thankful he was here.

At the appearance of the two warriors, the demons turned their attention away from Kyle and the boys and began a new strategy for warfare. They were joined by other demons, much more foul and ferocious creatures, flashing multiple layers of sharp teeth, ten-inch claws on every hand, and standing over seven feet tall. They arched their backs as Halecim and Jonah approached the pole where Beth was bound.

To combat them, the warrior angel and his sidekick moved stealthily, like Ninjas, in complete synchronisation as they swung their blades in unison at their attackers. As strong, thick claws were aimed at their heads and chest, they needed a strong grip to hold their swords tight and keep them from flying out of their hands.

Jonah came up against two attackers at once but he used a mixture of nifty moves, ducking and diving between the legs of these huge beasts and then jabbing them with quick, successive stabs of his sword. Halecim had attackers on three sides, trying to claw at him from every direction, but he was far too quick and skilful for them. As he swung his sword, he used his massive arms and strong wings to knock them all down. There was no room for mercy here and every thrust of the sword was targeted for a kill. Halecim swung his sword hard over his right shoulder and down towards the largest of the demons, slicing his arm clean off, continuing with an upswing motion as he rotated his hips clockwise and sliced his sword across his adversary's abdomen, cutting him into two halves. The high-pitched squeals were deafening but, ignoring them, Halecim quickly took out another demon whose deathly screams were followed by the last gasps of breath that came from one of Jonah's defeated rivals.

The two warriors stood back to back, with just two demons left to fight. Together they shouted a powerful war-cry, that Halecim had taught Jonah earlier, and then charged towards their enemy, frantically but accurately swinging their swords from side to side. They reached their adversaries at the same time and, with the first strike of their swords, forced their prey to cringe and bow out of the fight. Suddenly, in a puff of smoke, the demons disappeared.

Jonah stood for a second, revelling in the glory of victory.

Halecim quickly looked around the arena to see who else would appear. 'Concentrate,' he warned, snapping his fingers in front of Jonah's face trying to grab his attention. 'We don't have long. They'll be back soon, with reinforcements.'

This brought Jonah quickly back to reality and he headed towards Beth, hoping to rescue her. On his way, he felt compelled to stop and talk to Kyle and the group of three boys huddled on the ground.

'What…I mean, how did you…?'

'It's okay Jonah. I brought them here,' said Kyle.

'You?'

'Just obeying orders from my Commander-in-Chief,' said Kyle pointing towards Halecim who was still surveying the territory.

'Your commander! So, you're a…you're a…'

'That's right. Angel Kyle, at your service.'

'I knew it! I knew there was something different about you,' said Jonah, 'Right from the beginning.'

Then he turned to Nat. 'So, has Kyle been helping you too?'

'Yeah,' said Nat. 'But I have no idea what's happening now. Why are we even here?'

'We're in a battle between two worlds,' said Jonah. 'It's massive. And you don't want to stay in this place too long. It's a dark and evil world and we need to get out of here as quickly as possible.'

Nat looked bleakly at his brother and best friend, who were lying on the floor, still bleeding and with little life left in them.

'We'll get them out too,' said Jonah. 'I promise.'

Then he hurried towards the giant pole where his mum was tied. Beth tried hard to lift her head to see him. She did not have the strength to keep her head lifted for long, but managed a weak smile when she saw him there in front of her.

Jonah raised his sword to slice at the twisted, thick ropes that bound his mum. He wanted to set her free but, as soon as he tried, he was pulled back by a massive explosion that erupted behind him. The blast seemed to be coming from a dark hole behind them in the cave, hurling giant lumps of rock at high speeds towards the group of frightened humans on the ground.

Halecim was swiftly by their side and opened his gigantic wings to deflect the large stones flying in their direction. As quick as a flash, they were joined by another pair of wings. These were not as large or as strong as those of the chief warrior but Kyle's fine pair of feathered

259

wings were certainly powerful enough to protect his friends.

Jonah could see Nat was in complete shock at the revelation that his former trainer at the gym was really an angel. There was no time for explanations though. The smoke and cloud from the explosion of rock began to settle and, as they all looked up towards the core direction of the bang, hundreds of demon warriors were hovering above them. They seemed to be lining up in formation, ready for war.

Halecim formed a barricade with his wings on one side of the group and Kyle moved to the other side, keeping the humans protected in the middle. All their feathers were visibly twitching. Something was wrong and both Halecim and Kyle knew it. This was not about the fight immediately in front of them. It was about a far greater battle that was just about to begin in a parallel world.

# 24

There were strange stirrings in the deep hollows of the mountain: an air of excitement, almost celebration, as hundreds of demons and evil spirits flew around the tunnels and vast caves. The word was spreading quickly. Something amazing was happening in the world of humans and the underworld waited in anticipation for the event they thought they would never see.

The greatest threat to hell, and everything in it, was the Creator. He had the power to eliminate its strongholds with a single command. Never in their wildest dreams could all the evil creatures believe that the Creator's Son would live on earth as a human, but he did. Although fully human, he still had the powers of the Creator and therefore seemed undefeatable. Even their own master, the dark lord Vilde, had tried his best tricks to tempt him to sin and rebel but this man, who Jonah called the Storyteller, had always resisted the strongest attacks. Until now.

As they sped through hidden portals in the walls of Vilde's lair, spreading the news in hundreds and thousands of different locations all over the world, the demonic forces were ecstatic with the anticipation of their greatest enemy being overthrown, having his supernatural power stripped from him forever. The conversations that the demonic forces enjoyed were filled with stories of what life would be like when their nemesis was eliminated. They would never have to fear again that they would be defeated or face extinction. It had seemed an impossible dream but now, as the story was unfolding on earth and the Storyteller was beaten, there was hope that this could be the end of any restrictions on their operations.

All hell could break loose. Literally.

***

In the parallel world of two thousand years ago, the Storyteller was facing execution. He had been rejected by most of his followers, charged with treason, and sentenced to a terrible death.

The rulers of the time used the method of crucifixion as their killing tool. They nailed the hands and feet of convicted criminals to two heavy wooden blocks crossed together and left them there to die slowly, for days. This was the most painful and cruel form of punishment ever invented. Now the Storyteller faced this fate. He was thrown to the ground, landing heavily on the main beam of the cross. It was over six feet long and two feet in diameter – cracked, jagged and full of splinters. The executioner raised a hammer high in the air and placed the first eight-inch, dirty nail just above the wrist of the Storyteller's right hand. The hammer came down fast and hit the nail hard into his skin and bone. The soldier raised the hammer again and hit the nail until it was driven firmly through his wrist and into the wood. The Storyteller groaned in deep agony and then grimaced in anticipation as he waited for the hammer to smash the second nail into his left wrist. His cries of pain, as the nails were forced through his wrists and both his feet, were heard throughout the universe and beyond.

\*\*\*

Halecim and Kyle had been unaware of the evolving scenes unfolding in the parallel world as they embarked on their quests. Now, they were the first to hear the agonising cries of the Storyteller echoing through the depths of Vilde's lair. They were overwhelmed with fear and, although they did not know exactly what was happening on earth, they knew they could not stay.

Halecim looked at Jonah with pain and deep concern in his eyes. 'Jonah, I'm sorry, we have to leave you,' he said, beckoning to Kyle.

'What do you mean?'

'Our Master is in trouble. We have to go.'

'But...but...' Jonah pointed at the army they were about to fight. 'What about them?'

Halecim put his hand on Jonah's shoulder. He lowered his head towards his young friend and gently whispered, 'You are strong enough now. You can win this battle without me. Have faith my friend. Believe.'

Then Kyle pulled a spare sword out from between his wings and gave it to Nat.

'Take it. You're going to need to fight too.'

In an instant, Halecim and Kyle disappeared.

Jonah paused briefly, turned to look at his mum, and then reached out to grasp Nat's hand. They pulled together for a man-hug before turning towards their opponents. Raising their swords, they moved forward with determination on their faces, into battle.

Nat had never brandished a sword before but he was very familiar with a variety of other weapons. He stood firm, close to Jonah, ready to fight for their lives. The smaller demons came towards them first. They were about four feet high and hair covered their distorted bodies in such a way that it was hard to tell where their limbs were supposed to be. They did not have swords but heavy, wooden clubs like primitive cave men. Jonah and Nat did not want to find out what being hit with a club felt like, so they made sure that every blow and strike of their swords was effective and deadly. Their aim was accurate and every demon that lost its battle dissolved into fragments as the angelic, crafted swords ripped through their bodies. Jonah was not sure if these creatures were simply teleporting themselves to another part of the underworld, but each one that disappeared was one less enemy to fight.

With Nat's support, Jonah ploughed through the first thirty beasts without any trouble. He was using the training he had received from Halecim and Kyle, while Nat used the street skills that he had developed over years of ruling the gangs on the estate. The two young warriors worked well together to fend off the enemy, as though they had been fight-buddies for years. It was surprising how easy it was to defeat a demon with the weapons of belief and unity.

When the small demons had all disappeared, a larger group of about fifty demons arrived. These were far more ferocious. They snarled like rabid dogs with razor-sharp teeth and thick, pointed claws. Jonah and Nat stood back-to-back for this fight, so they could cover every angle of attack, while the dog-demons either crouched low to the ground or jumped up high to try and bite their throats. The beasts had formed themselves into pairs and their coordinated attacks came fast and furiously. As soon as one pair of dog-demons had been struck and then evaporated, the next pair attacked.

Jonah and Nat had worked their way through about half of the pack when they began to realise the battle strategy had changed. The next pair of demons were not approaching as usual. Instead they remained still and silent, in their crouching positions, as if they were waiting for new orders. The atmosphere in the cave was intense and Jonah and Nat stood close to each other, trying to figure out what was going on. They presumed that reinforcements had been called, worthy opponents who would be better able to tackle these two humans who had fought with such power and were still standing. But Jonah felt uneasy about the silence. What, or who, were their enemies waiting for? How long could they keep fighting? It was already a miracle that he and Nat were still in one piece.

All they could do was hope Halecim and Kyle would return soon. If they were going to return.

# 25

The two warrior angels hovering in the sky looked down on the hill outside the walled city. Their Master was nailed to a cross, hung on public display, to be mocked and humiliated by those he came to save.

The soldiers on the hill were happy to be entertained by this helpless, weak man, who took all the sadistic punishment and torture that they threw at him. Some mocked and taunted him as they struck him on the head with long walking sticks, spat at him, and punched his sides. Some even pretended to bow down to the one who dared to call himself the 'King of the Jews'.

Halecim was not ready for defeat. He gave out a commanding call for his army and the sky was suddenly filled with a multitude of angels. They assembled in regimental order, all their swords drawn, ready to rescue their Lord. All they needed was their Master, or his father the Creator, to give the word and they would swoop down and rescue him. Then they could slaughter all the mocking soldiers who put him on this gruesome deathbed of wood and nails.

Halecim and Kyle hovered in the clouds, powerless to do anything without the order from above. They waited, in anticipation and concern for their Master, but no command to rescue him ever came. Instead they watched, helpless, as he was taunted by the humans, who put sponges soaked with sour drinks onto their sticks and pushed them into his face. They heard him cry out in pain; they heard him call to his father for help; they heard him ask why had he been abandoned?

They could not believe what they were hearing. A vast army of angels covered the skies waiting to save their Master. They had not abandoned him. They had not given up but, without the order from the Creator, there was nothing they could do. They watched their Master take his final breath and die, his body slumped, only held on the wooden cross by the nails in his hands and feet. They could not understand why this had been allowed to happen. All they could do was watch as he was lowered from the cross and carried away to a tomb, to be buried. His body was wrapped in cloth and placed in a small cave with a huge stone pushed over the entrance, to stop anyone reaching him.

A sorrowful silence filled the skies. Nothing could be heard, not even the sound of wings flapping in the breeze. It was the worst day in history.

\*\*\*

A massive cheer erupted in the cave. It was a victory cry from the vast army of demonic spirits, jubilant at their conquest in the everlasting war of evil against good. The deafening noise of these triumphant cries continued for what seemed like hours.

Jonah and Nat were still waiting in the dim light of the cave for their enemy to strike, but instead they watched as, one by one, the demons slinked away from the centre of the lair towards the sounds of celebration. Very soon the humans were alone. They looked at each other, puzzled but relieved. It was a good opportunity to look around and assess their situation.

Nat ran over to check on Banksi and Dan who both lay lifeless on the ground. It was not looking good for them. They were still losing a lot of blood, although at least they were still breathing.

Jonah wanted to help them too, but he was also acutely aware that his mother remained a prisoner in the lair, tied to the stake that kept her hostage. He knew he had to take advantage of this sudden pause in the warfare to cut her free. He crossed carefully over to where Beth was leaning against the base of the pole, with her hands tied above her head and her legs tucked beneath her. She seemed very frail and barely aware that her son was using his sword to cut through the thick cords that bound her. This time, with no resistance from the demons, Jonah was able to successfully complete the task and set her free. He then tried to help Beth move away from the stake.

Battered and bruised, physically and emotionally, Beth was too weak to walk. She had to keep rubbing her legs as they ached with cramp from being kept in the same position for days. Still, she managed to reach out a hand towards her son. When Jonah took it, she looked at him with a grateful smile. For a moment she let him put his arms around her and hug her tight.

The atmosphere in the lair began to change. Sounds of jubilation and cheering in the distance had faded. Instead, the dog-demons were beginning to return with other creatures – some small, others gigantic, but all horribly disfigured. They kept their noses to the ground, grovelling behind a swirling mass of cloth, as a towering figure in a long black robe emerged. There was the most disgusting smell, like a rat's carcass rotting in the sun, as the faceless creature spread his cloak.

Jonah's legs started to shake; sweat rolled down his face.

'What is it?' said Nat, staring in horror at the creature.

Jonah could hardly breathe but he managed to whisper, 'This is my worst enemy...Theda... the chief warrior in Vilde's army. He's been chasing me for a long time. He's the one who kidnapped my mum and brought her here. Pure evil.'

'I'm not surprised you fought back when my gang attacked you, if this is what you've been running from,' said Nat, his voice filled with fear.

As Theda moved closer to his targets, the surrounding demons started going wild with excitement. Jonah knew he had to move swiftly to protect the boys and stand between them and this frenzied force of darkness. Courage swelled in his heart and his arms tensed, as he gripped his sword tightly and leaned over to grab Nat's sword too.

When Nat tried to stop him, Jonah pushed him away. 'No, he's after me, not you. Don't get involved. If you fight Theda and lose, you die. Forever.'

Theda moved slowly towards Jonah, taking his time to create an atmosphere of menace. Over the centuries, since the universe began, he had approached his prey in many terrifying ways; sometimes instantly without any warning; sometimes over a prolonged, torturous time of suffering. Some people knew he was coming for them and almost expected him to visit, whilst others were in complete shock that their life was finally up. The only inevitable thing in the created world was that sooner or later everyone would meet him and die.

Theda looked around the great cave with his hands held high, encouraging his companions to make some noise. He looked full of glee that finally he had reached Jonah, without Halecim there to protect him. At last, he could prove himself a worthy supreme warrior for Vilde. He stood arrogantly and bellowed in a deep, grizzly voice, 'Today we have won the war. Today our enemy, Son of the Creator, is dead.'

A rapturous roar ripped through the underworld as millions of evil spirits and demonic forces claimed their victory.

This was the first time that Jonah realised that all the commotion in the lair was about the Storyteller – the mild, caring and compassionate man he had met on his journeys through the Doorway. Over time, he had come to believe in the uniqueness and special qualities of this

271

man. He had seen him perform miracles, heal people, and even bring a little girl back from the dead. Now, Jonah was furious that the demons were celebrating the death of the amazing man who had become his friend. He had to do something to strike back. He began to raise both the swords in his hands and prepare his feet for charging at his enemies, when suddenly he heard a voice whisper gently in his ear, 'Jonah, put down your weapons. This is my fight.'

He turned around quickly but no-one was there. Mystified, he turned back to see Theda still revelling in his victory.

Suddenly, as if from nowhere, a man appeared behind Theda. 'Are you sure I'm dead?' asked the man, quietly.

Theda jumped into the air in shock and horror, shouting 'No. NO. How can it be?'

Jonah was amazed. It was the Storyteller.

A loud gasp went out from all the demons in the great cave, a fearful noise that soon replaced the sounds of earlier celebrations. Theda drew his sword from its sheath and raised it high above his head with both hands. The Storyteller raised his right arm towards Theda and, as he did, the sleeve of his robe fell back to reveal the hole in his hand where, only a few hours earlier, a nail had pinned him to the cross.

Theda's sword came crashing down with great power but stopped a few millimetres away from the Storyteller's outstretched arm. Theda tried to force it down further but, as he tried to push hard on the blade, he failed to see his opponent lift his left hand slowly. Too late, Theda looked up as a bolt of lightning darted from his enemy's palm, striking him in the stomach. It sent him flying backwards and he crashed to the ground.

Jonah and Nat were about to cheer but were silenced as Theda's army drew their weapons to assist their chief. The demons raised sharpened swords, knives, metal bars and claws to attack the Storyteller but, before any weapon could strike, they were interrupted by a flash of blinding light. The ceiling of the giant lair was transformed, from its charcoal black and garish reds of constant fire, into a bright white vision of splendour.

Halecim and Kyle had returned with their warriors.

The army of angels filled the cave in a giant cloud above the demons, swords ready to protect and serve their Master in his ultimate battle with Theda, and to protect the humans in their care.

Angels and demons watched as Theda tried everything that he could do to strike the Storyteller. Nothing worked. His repeated efforts, to get up and fight, constantly failed. While the Storyteller stood calm and invincible, Theda was tasting defeat. He had never lost before. Never. This was tearing him apart. He looked around the cave for inspiration, realising that the army of demons were trapped by the cloud of angels above them.

Then a rumble of something that sounded like thunder began to echo around the cave walls and a blast of scorching wind swept through the lair like a tornado. The army of demons shook violently when they saw it and crowded around the sweeping column of fire, bowing their heads to the ground.

'All hail Vilde,' came the cry that resounded through the arena.

As Theda dared to glance upwards, he saw Vilde thundering down a giant, black staircase suspended in the flames. Their eyes met and, in that moment, the dark lord looked at his chief warrior in absolute disgust. Then, with a terrible sneer, he spiralled back into the column of fire and left the lair as quickly as he had come. Deserted by his master, Theda fell for the final time.

The Storyteller approached the trembling creature and placed his right foot on the defeated demon's chest.

'You have been conquered, Theda. You have no hold over me anymore and therefore you have no hold over my followers. Vilde has escaped for now because today is not his time. Our battle will come later. Until that day, you will release anyone from your stronghold when I tell you. Do you understand?'

Theda nodded quietly.

'You can start with my five friends over there,' said the Storyteller, with the utmost authority.

Theda stood to his feet, embarrassed and afraid, and picked up his sword. Halecim flew at lightning speed towards him, fearing for an attack on his Master, but Theda quietly put the sword back in his belt and speedily left the cave. As soon as he had gone, the rest of his army left too and, minutes later, all was calm in the cave. The heavy cloak of darkness had gone.

The Storyteller walked over to Banksi and Dan and placed his hands on their heads. Immediately, the bleeding stopped. Amazed, the lads woke to discover their wounds were healed.

'How did we get here?' said Dan, completely baffled.

'Yeah, where...where are we?' said Banksi.

'Your brother will explain,' said the Storyteller.

Nat looked lost for words. He kept staring in bewilderment at the scene before his eyes. Not only did the two gang members look well, they seemed healthier than he had ever seen them look before.

Leaving the boys to catch up on their news, the Storyteller crossed over to Beth and reached out his hand to help her. As soon as he held her palm, her injuries were healed and she sprang to her feet with a surge of energy.

'How do you feel?' asked the Storyteller, looking at her with a warm smile.

'I feel like there's a lightness flooding through my body. I've never felt so... peaceful,' said Beth.

'I am glad you feel at peace. I have not removed the memories of your captivity, although I have taken out the sting of any pain they may cause. For the moment, it is important that you can remember where you have been, so that you can help Jonah recover from his journey and for you both to have a more hopeful future.'

'Thank you,' said Beth. 'I will never forget this moment.' She put her arms around the Storyteller believing, in this brief experience, that he was special; he seemed to know everything about her and she could feel that he loved her just as she was.

The Storyteller then walked over to Jonah and placed his hands on his shoulders. 'You have proved yourself a brave young man. Well done.'

Jonah could hardly speak. He felt overwhelmed by a mixture of sadness, guilt and relief.

'I am sorry for not believing in you for so long. Please forgive me,' he said, quietly and with his head bowed low.

'I do forgive you and always will, whenever you ask. Although it is true that forgiveness is the hardest thing in creation, because we remember the pain. I have walked on earth as a man and I understand, more than you know, the difficulties you face and the choices you have had to make along the way. You have been on a difficult journey and I am very pleased that you have stuck with it and not given up. I also know you have an earthly father who wants to be forgiven by you.'

Jonah gasped. How did the Storyteller know his dad?

'I have spent time with him too, recently, and his journey has been just as challenging as yours.'

Jonah's face lit up, as if a lightbulb had been turned on in his heart, when he realised this was the man his dad had been trying to tell him about that night they met in the park.

'Forgiveness starts by realising there is hope that a relationship can be restored,' said the Storyteller. 'I believe you and your father can have that hope too.' Then he put his arms around Jonah and gave him a huge hug.

When Jonah finally looked up, he could see that everyone else was smiling.

# 26

It was a strange journey. No-one really knew how they arrived. One moment Jonah, Banksi, Dan, Nat and Beth were huddled together in a tight group in Vilde's underworld; the next, they were standing in an open space, full of greenery. A cool breeze was blowing, filled with the smell of earth, and they saw they were standing in the small field on the edge of their home town.

As Jonah looked at the path, that led along the edge of the river, he recognised the pile of stones that had once been the bridge that crossed the river to the pub. The memories came flooding back. The last time he had stood here, he had witnessed the bridge collapsing and the terrifying sight of his mother sinking into the ground, after he lost his frantic fist-fight with Theda. Now, no one was trying to capture or kill them. Instead the Storyteller, Halecim and Kyle were there to protect them. Jonah felt incredibly happy to be alive.

He was not the only one. For the five humans standing in the field, their journey had been a remarkable experience which none of them would ever forget. They had been through a lot, individually and together, but having come out of it in one piece, they did not want their adventure to end.

The Storyteller was the first to speak, breaking the silence. 'Now we have brought you all safely home, it is time for us to say our goodbyes.'

Everyone looked sad at this announcement.

'Are you all going?' asked Jonah, looking at Halecim.

His giant friend nodded.

'Don't worry, Jonah,' said the Storyteller. 'I'll make sure Halecim keeps an eye on you, and pops down to see you from time to time. He has learned a lot from you. After all,' he continued with a smile, 'he has never had the pleasure of being human.'

'Yes, you have been a challenge, I must admit,' said Halecim, looking straight into Jonah's eyes. 'But it has been a pleasure and an honour to be your protector and companion. I don't have too many human friends – too busy fighting the baddies – so I'm very glad you were the one chosen for me to spend time with.'

Jonah struggled to get his words out, due to the big lump in his throat. 'It's me that needs to be thankful,' he finally said. 'I know I've not been easy to take on, quite stroppy at times, but your patience and wisdom have helped me, more than you know. I will never forget you my friend.'

While Halecim and Jonah hugged each other tightly, Nat approached Kyle.

'Are you going too?' he asked, disappointed to be losing his mentor.

'I am. My time on earth has ended.'

'But you can't go. I mean…what about the gym?'

'Oh, it doesn't end here, you know,' said Kyle with a massive grin as he stretched out his hand and gave Nat a bunch of keys. 'The gym's yours now. Do something positive with it.'

Nat could hardly believe it.

'You can get Dan and Banksi to help you,' Kyle continued. 'It will be up to you all to run the estate in a positive way from now on, giving people the opportunity to grow and support each other, not fight and destroy.'

Nat was overwhelmed. 'Thank you, Kyle…thank you for everything,' he finally managed to say, 'I won't let you down.' Then he turned towards Banksi and Dan, shaking the keys in his hand. 'The gym's ours, lads. We've been given a chance to make a difference on the estate and change our own little world for the better.'

The former bad-boys were just as stunned as Nat. For all of them, it was difficult to say goodbye to Kyle but, after hugs and farewells were shared between everyone, the Storyteller signalled to his angel warriors that it was time to leave.

Jonah found this the hardest moment. He did not want to say goodbye to the man he now trusted more than anyone in the world.

As if he could read his thoughts, the Storyteller turned to Jonah and said gently, 'Don't be sad. I may not be visible to you after we leave but that does not mean I will not be around. We can still talk and share together, just not face to face. Our spirits can always connect. And as your journey continues, now and throughout your life, you will never be alone when you face trials and challenges. For I will always be with you, to the very end. My death and resurrection have made it possible for you, and the whole of humanity, to have a relationship with me and my father the Creator, whenever you want it.'

Jonah smiled at the thought of a relationship with someone who was a loving, caring father. He held onto that thought while the group of heavenly beings slowly disappeared into the mist, leaving him standing alone with the others in the empty field.

'What do we do now?' said Dan. 'It's not going to be easy to walk back into our old lives as if nothing has happened.'

'That's right. We left everything in such a mess,' said Banksi, worried about the consequences of his actions.

'Well, one thing that this journey has shown us is that nothing is easy but all things are possible,' said Nat. 'I believe we can do this. But if we are going to make a difference to the others who live on our estate, we need to lead by example, however tough that's going to be.'

'That's alright for you to say,' said Banksi. 'You're not going to get arrested for causing a riot.'

'It wasn't just you, Banksi,' said Dan. 'We were both wrong in how we reacted. Our desire to replace Nat as king of the block caused a lot of people to get hurt. It was my fault too.'

'We have to accept that all of our actions were wrong,' said Nat. 'That means we're going to have to make a conscious effort to apologise to everyone we've hurt and use the money from the gym to pay for any repairs that are needed. Then, if we do have to face the 'time for the crime' we'll do it together.'

Banksi still looked worried but nodded his head in agreement. 'As long as I don't have to go through this alone.'

As if from nowhere, an unexpected voice, but one they all recognised, breathed like as whisper caught in the breeze.

'From this day forward, you will never be alone. I will be with all of you...until the end of your days, and beyond.'

Everyone looked around, trying to catch a glimpse of the Storyteller. They heard his voice and knew he was with them, even though they could no longer see him. It filled them all with hope.

Banksi, Dan and Nat began to walk towards the centre of town, arms around each other's shoulders, ready to take on the world.

'I think it's time for us to go home too,' said Beth, looking at Jonah.

'That sounds good. I'm shattered,' said Jonah.

Beth linked her left arm through Jonah's right arm, holding on tightly. 'I just want you to know that your courage, in rescuing us all, has made me so happy. I love you son and I'm proud of you. Really proud.'

'I love you too mum. But we need to talk about...' He stopped, unsure how to say it.

'It's okay,' said Beth, 'I know. It's time we talked about your Dad…what we're going to do. Maybe build a few bridges?'

'Yes. Let's do that,' said Jonah, surprised at how happy he felt. 'Let's go and live the life the Storyteller wants us to live.'

They joined the others in making their way home. As they did, a sense of joy and excitement filled them all. Together they would work to create a better future for everyone on the estate. Together they would make a difference.

And they would start by sharing their story, with anyone who would listen.

Printed in Poland
by Amazon Fulfillment
Poland Sp. z o.o., Wrocław

54645566R00169